BURIED WITHIN

A Haunting Anthology

Written by University Students

Burried Within: A Haunting Anthology by Book Editing and Design I&II.

Published by BookBaby in 2023.

Artwork curtosey of Jeanri Bosch.

Cover design by Jeanri Bosch and Sophia Lewis.

Layout by Cryptid Parke and Megan Farmer.

Typography: Atkinson Hyperlegible, Carta Marina.

Printed in the United States.

To those before
To those after
To us now
And to those beyond
Seen or unseen
Here but not here

The Midnight Club,
Mike Flanagan

We would like to express our deepest thanks to the generous donations from the families of Murrayhill Martial Arts, to those who bought items from our craft fair, to Kat Postma and the rest of the English Department at Pacific University, to those who inspire and support us, and to the ghosts that haunt us.

All proceeds from the sale of this book will benefit the Mental Health and Addiction Association of Oregon.

This book was written on Kalapuyan land.

EDITORIAL MASTHEAD

Layout and Design

Cryptid Parke

Megan Farmer

Emma Blackwell

Drew Sherman

Cover Art

Jean-Marie Bosch

Sophia Lewis

Reigen Komagata

Marketing and Fundraising

Haley Taylor

Gracie Shoemaker

Riley Reynolds

Emotional Support Dog

Marley

CONTENTS

SPOOKY METER

Each piece is given a rating out of five ghosts. Various factors go into the spooky meter rating, such as emotional intesnity, on-page violence/gore, and overall ghastliness of the piece.

Additionally, each piece has been given specific content warnings when applicable.

FOREWORDS

Over half of the writers in this anthology are not pursuing creative writing at the academic level. Some are creative writing majors. Others used to write as a child. Others write recreationally. Others have never written creatively before at all. What unites us, though, is the idea that each and every one of us is haunted, and we feel an obligation to speak about it.

The writers in this beautifully eerie collection interrogate what lies in our shadows. In these pages, you will find murder mysteries, tea parties, letters, confessions, allegories, and revelations, each coming to an understanding of how we all exist in a haunted world, and how it is up to us to choose how we move forward. Our ghosts will always haunt us, but there are ways in which we may find peace.

Josie Kochendorfer
Writer & Professor of English

Writing has always been something like a haunting to me since I was a child. Language was the monster in my closet, and it filled so many of my fears and nightmares. Between dyslexia and hearing problems, I was often told writing was never going to be part of my daily life even when I was passionate about it. Being able to overcome these ghosts took a lot of time and commitment. Getting to the point of teaching and guiding those with writing is an even bigger accomplishment! I came into this process with passion and experience to support those around me and avoid creating negative experiences with those I was working with.

In the past, I had taken this class with Josie and fell deeper in love with creating books. Because of this, I came back to this class, but as a teacher's assistant this time. I had the wonderful experience of helping the professor, Josie, and my peers with creating and designing the book. Since we only had about three months to complete this book, when most books take over a year, it was a lot of work and stress. During this time I was able to support and get closer with all the editors and writers. Being a part of the creation of this book was one of the most heartwarming and wonderful experiences. Fostering and creating a space with creativity and growth was one of the biggest goals. Growth was not just seen in the students but instead was felt around the whole room.

There were many hardships that this group went through before we were able to have a final product. On top of creating pieces, editing, layout, and cover design, we were also able to fundraise over a thousand dollars to publish our book. A whole group of our editors planned and executed our advertising and fundraising. To do this we worked as a group to create wonderful things to sell at a craft fair we hosted. Working with the editors, we also wanted to ensure that the book we created was accessible to many people. This included a long discussion about things like font choice, font size, and even layout designs. Because of this, we decided to go with the font that was created by the Braille Institute. Atkinson Hyperlegible was created to support people with low vision but is also great for people with disabilities.

Being able to see this class as a student and then later as one of the teachers was a great experience. The haunting pieces in this book will definitely leave a lasting impression, just like the community that was created when preparing this book. Thank you to everyone who made this possible and supported all of us during this creative time. And thank you, especially to Josie Kochendorfer. She is one of the best teachers and mentors during my time in college and will forever be part of my inspiration and teaching philosophy.

Lexzi Caso
Educator & Teaching Assistant

CASE FILE 936

CRYPTID PARKE

CONTENT WARNINGS:

Cancer, discussions of death

Department of Supernatural Research
February 27, 2019
ATTENTION: Director Maura Blake
SUBJECT: Evidence of paranormal interaction with the physical world
COMMITTEE: Hauntings Investigation

EXPLANATION:
A eulogy from the funeral of Ms. Delilah Jenkins delivered by the deceased's friend, Ms. Siobhan Leeroy was recently recovered by our field investigation and research team. The document appears to be an original copy of the printed eulogy from the funeral with hand-written annotations from the deceased Delilah Jenkins. The funeral was held nearly a year ago, on April 5th, 2018. See scanned document below for further details.

COMMENTS:
- Attempts to contact Ms. Jenkins' living family or Ms. Leeroy have been unsuccessful.
- Requesting that the Spiritual Communication Committee attempt to make contact with Ms. Jenkins.
- Other documents recovered with information on Ms. Jenkins failed to display similar annotations.
- Annotations appear to be light hearted, limited risk for a malicious haunting.

Friends and family, we are gathered here today to remember the life of my beloved friend, Delilah Jenkins.

A wise woman once told me that "there is

I can practically hear your grandma saying this

so much more to life than just going through the motions day by day, you must put effort into actually living." There is no one else I have met that put as much effort into living as Delilah.

God, that was so long ago

Delilah and I met in 10th grade when I transferred to Barlo High School. My father had recently died, and my mother and I were struggling to make ends meet. Delilah was a

Aww you're so sweet (& a cheesy dork)

breath of fresh air in a world that was plagued with darkness. I'll never forget what she said when she walked up to me on my first day to show me around:

I can't believe you remember this, you're such a loser

"Hi there, I'm Delilah! It's awesome to meet you. I heard that things have been rough, and even though we just met, I hope that I can be a pillar of support for you."

we're besties forever

And the rest is history. From that day forward, we were inseparable. She was a beacon of hope in my darkness, and I can say with full confidence that I was not the only one who was touched by her kindness. But, that's

Damn right lol
This is MY funeral

enough about me. We're here for Delilah.

Our beloved Delilah Marie Jenkins was born

Bro I didn't even know I was born in MN

on October 13th, 1993 in Rochester, Minnesota as the only child of Suzanna and Lloyd Jenkins. In her youth, Delilah lived in Barlo, Wisconsin, and after finishing high school she moved to Washington to attend Mountainview University. Delilah is survived by her parents, Suzanna and Lloyd, her maternal grandmother and paternal grandmother, Lilliana and Shahid, and all of the beloved family and friends who have come to

I hope they're doing alright,
they shouldn't have to deal with this

show their love for her today.

No one should have to deal with their kid dying this young

Delilah was taken from us far too young,

That's corny as hell

only 24 years old. She had so much of her life

ahead of her, but we can say with certainty that

she lived what little life she had to the absolute

I guess I did

fullest. At 21 she graduated from Mounainview

University with a degree in biochemistry, and

moved on to Mercy Lloyd University to complete

her masters program in molecular biology.

Unfortunately, she was unable to complete the

Absolute hypocrites

program before passing, but Mercy Lloyd has

been kind enough to award her the degree

regardless due to her dedication and spirit.

where was this energy when I was actively dying of cancer?

Delilah lived life with a joy that was

unparalleled by anyone else. She was the kindest

person I've ever met, and the best friend I could

I should be the one thanking you

possibly ask for. Thank you all for being here to

give her the beautiful send off that she deserves.

You never left my side through it all, and I'm forever grateful for you

Delilah, if you are here, I hope you know

that we all love you so very much, and that our

lives would not have been the same without you.

I miss you so much Lilah-girl. You better be waiting up there with a mug of tea for me when my time comes.

Thank you all.

I miss you so much, Siobhan
Keep on fighting the good fight & shine so bright sweet girl

I Love You
—Delilah

Up At 3 AM

Jeanri Bosch

Content Warnings:
Blood, gore, nightmares

I was trying to wake him by scratching at his skin, to warn him about what was coming from the other room. I could barely move, barely see, I was scared. But each time I fell asleep again, waking up to repeat the scratching.

For as long as I can remember, I've had some wacky dreams. I have found myself in vastly different worlds and scenarios. Throughout my life, dreams have always fascinated me. At one point, I had started sending voice notes of my dreams to my friends, but the voice notes were unorganized and hard to understand with my half-asleep rambling. So when I was around sixteen, I started making my voice notes into stories in a dream journal. My dream journal consisted of about forty-five pages and would have more, but I haven't written in a long time. I can't seem to remember my dreams as vividly as I used to. My dreams used to be a lot more frequent and a lot less nightmare-esque. They were more interesting than day to day life, and I enjoyed the adrenaline and surrealism that they provided. I felt like they were fueling my imagination and daydreams during the daytime.

Digging its claws into my calves and pulling me. As a

of blood followed it pulled me into the unknown, and away from the waking world.

My dreams had the tendency to feed into my obsessions, like when I went grocery shopping with fictional characters from whichever show I binge-watched at the time, or finding myself on a beach with a favorite K-pop band. I was so interested in my dreams and obsessions, I started seeing videos about it on social media. The videos were on how to go to fictional worlds in your dreams and how to have characters visit you in your dreams. About how you can create real relationships with these characters. These videos were largely about manifesting these dream visits, and multiple people had step-by-step instructions on how to succeed. I never believed what they were saying. I was no longer interested in finding meanings for my dreams. My feelings around dreams and obsessions are that the more you think of a topic or person during the day, the more likely they will be in your dreams. Later, this was proven kind of true when I got to college. In my freshman year, I took a psychology class that explained how dreams are more about moving your short-term memory into long-term memory.

Ragdoll puppets were recreating the previous night's event while she dealt with the issue of all her teeth falling out.

More often than not, I wouldn't consider my dreams nightmares or good dreams. Usually they are so random that they don't really fit into either category. I'm sure that if I could remember all my dreams I've ever had, I'd be able to decide which are good and which are bad. However, since I didn't care why I had a dream where my teeth fell out or what it meant that there was a small sparkly man standing next to a food truck, I simply tried to remember and enjoy the dreams that I could. I have more dreams when sleeping on my back. I remember many moments of purposefully going to sleep on my back, hoping to have more interesting dreams. It has also given me more lucid dreams. These are dreams where I could feel everything that is happening to me. Could feel bugs crawling around under my skin. Or the warmth of the sun shining through leaves. I also have a lot more control in lucid dreams. I'm more aware that they are dreams, so I can wake myself up if my dream goes sour.

It was almost peaceful in the warehouse. Until it started raining blood and bugs while you realized you were trapped in a building.

Lucid dreams have caused me to lay awake between three and five in the morning. The lucid dreams that woke me are those where I am not in control of my own body. Or others were touching me in ways I didn't want to be touched. Dreams where chunks of my body were ripped off in one way or another. Even one where I thought I had died. I am lucky enough to have taught myself how to wake up from these dreams whenever they become more unpleasant than I can bear. I discovered this when I was 10 years old, and had a looping nightmare of a witch chasing me. Waking myself up kind of feels like rolling my eyes really, really far back into my head. Often after I wake myself, I need to "reset" my brain, basically just not allowing myself to fall back asleep immediately, to stop thinking about the dream, and to usually chug some water. This has helped so I don't have the same dream when I fall asleep again. My resetting process is mainly just me staring at my phone screen for about 2 hours till I'm no longer thinking about the dream. I think my relationship with my dreams started changing around this time. Once I started gaining more control of my dreams, they became more intense, and were harder to remember. After that, waking myself up didn't always go as planned. On the odd occasion, I got sleep paralysis.

Knocking him out and dragging him into a forest with help from your family and two large dogs was probably the easy part. The hard part was when he woke up halfway through being burnt and you had to kill him with your bare hands.

Whenever I could only half wake myself, I would get sleep paralysis. With my sleep paralysis, I am unable to move and I am only half awake. I am able to comprehend what's happening around me, but unable to move. There's usually some sort of unwanted thing there with me, whether that be a creepy little girl in a corner, or my arm appearing to be gone. A few weeks ago, I started seeing videos on folklore horror stories, and it fully freaked me out. That night, I woke up with sleep paralysis several times. I wasn't able to fully wake up and reset after having sleep paralysis, so the dream and sleep paralysis kept looping. With sleep paralysis like that, I have, on more than one occasion, woken up with a panic attack, gasping for air while my head still spins with sleep. Although it's scary, I wouldn't trade lucid dreaming to no longer have sleep paralysis. I think I enjoy being thrown into the surrealism and adrenaline of lucid dreams too much for that.

The father was carrying the dead, charred body of his daughter. He was on a beach vacation with the rest of the family.

Currently, I am not having nearly as many interesting dreams as I was a few years ago, and the ones I do have are quickly forgotten. For the most part, I'm really only getting scary sleep paralysis ones. I've started forgetting them a lot sooner, if I even remember them at all. A few months ago, I almost gave my boyfriend a heart attack in the middle of the night. I was still asleep and don't remember a thing, though he claims that I started screaming and thrashing around like I was being exorcized. I wish I knew why I don't have as many dreams as I used to, I quite enjoyed having them frequently. Maybe I haven't been having as many since I haven't been as obsessed with characters or shows recently. I've been more obsessed with my everyday life. There have been so many changes in my life over the past few years. I've moved out of my parents' house and started college, gotten into my first serious relationship, and essentially stopped eating meat and drinking fizzy drinks. All good changes, since I'm not seventeen anymore. As my life continues to change and grow, I look forward to seeing how my dream habits change. I kind of hope they go back to the absurd seventeen-year-old ones.

I lay on the floor in a ball, my hands covering my ears. But nothing could help with the sounds of bodies crunching on pavement. My hands could not block out people yelling and police sirens.

LIVING IN THE ECHOES

HALEY TAYLOR

I don't believe in ghosts. At least, not the spirits that people always talk about. Not the ones that inhabit old houses or the ones that make the upstairs curtains move or the ones that hang out in cemeteries. The dead aren't hanging onto life, desperately trying to communicate with us; they've moved on. The living can haunt themselves all on their own.

"Stacy!" my best friend calls, rushing up to me in the hallway before class.

I look up from my book, leaning against the wall outside my first period. "Hi, Olive." I smile at her, ignoring the ghost hovering over her shoulder. Her own personal ghost, though 'ghost' isn't really the right word for it. It's Olive, albeit a transparent and much grumpier version of her. I call them echoes and, as far as I know, I'm the only one that sees them.

The grin on her face is a mile wide. "You will never believe what just happened!"

I laugh as she bounces up and down. "Are you going to tell me or what?" Her echo rolls its eyes at me, though I don't acknowledge it. Usually echoes don't notice me, but Olive's likes to make mocking faces at me when it thinks I'm not looking.

"Duncan asked me to prom!" She squeals, unable to contain her excitement.

My heart sinks, but I do my best to maintain my smile. She's been crushing on Duncan for weeks. Any other day I'd be thrilled, but now I'm the only one in our friend group without a date to senior prom. "That's great, Olive." I try to keep my voice upbeat so that I don't ruin her happiness, but the disappointment seeps through.

Olive notices and sighs sympathetically. Her echo sticks out its tongue. "There's still time for someone to ask you."

I shake my head. "Prom is in two days. If someone was going to ask me, they would've done it by now."

She makes a face and waves her hand. "Who needs a date to prom anyway, right?"

I give her one of my patented *are-you-kidding-me* looks, which she ignores.

"We're all going as a big group. It's going to be fun no matter what."

I imagine it: all my friends, their dates, and me. Standing awkwardly off to the side while they get couple photos. Watching on the sidelines while everyone slow-dances with their date. I'll be the thirteenth wheel, so beyond unnecessary.

"Maybe I just won't go." I say the words slowly, bracing myself for her reaction.

Her echo grins gleefully and whispers in Olive's ear. I can't make out the words; I just hear a faint buzzing. Whatever it's telling her isn't going to be good. In the six years since I started seeing echoes, I haven't heard them say a kind word about anyone.

"You have to go!" she exclaims, looking outraged. "Are you crazy? This is senior prom. You can't miss your senior prom." I shrug, and she whacks my shoulder. "Come on, Stacy, are you serious? You promised you would come this time."

I shift awkwardly. Olive has been begging me to go to

a school dance with the group ever since I moved here, and each time I back out at the last second. I promised her this time would be different.

Some friend she is, the echo announces to Olive, shooting me a nasty grin. *She doesn't care about you.*

I open my mouth to argue with the echo, but I know I can't. Olive doesn't know it's there, and she'll think I'm crazy, just like everyone at my old school did. It's been two years, but even now the memory of their judging eyes makes my skin crawl.

I know I'm letting Olive down, and I feel guilty about it, I do. I know she couldn't care less whether a guy likes me, but it's our other friends, Olive's friends, that I know will judge me. I've heard the nasty things their echoes say about me. I convinced myself it wouldn't be so bad if Olive and I both didn't have dates, that I could hang out with her the whole time, but now it's just me. I'll be miserable by myself.

"Fine," Olive says, breaking the silence as the bell rings. She glares at me. "Don't go. But don't expect me to miss you." She storms down the hallway without a second glance.

I resist the urge to plug my ears as I make my way to fourth period, not that it would do much good. Even if I could block out all the sounds in the real world, I would still hear the echoes, who always scream the loudest in the hallways.

I try desperately to tune them out, but I only make it a few steps before their chattering floods my brain. *You're ugly. You're stupid. No one likes you. You'll never amount to anything. You're going to let everyone down.* They aren't talking to me, but their words bleed through the cracks in my brain, taking over like a parasite. Pressure grows inside my head and a buzz fills my ears until they ache.

Their sentences overlap each other until all that remains is unbearable, depressing noise. I want to scream or cry, anything to make it all stop. Only experience keeps me from having a panic attack.

I realize that I'm standing still in the hallway, and I do my best to steady my breathing. It's not true, I remind myself. Nothing that the echoes say is true. Just let it go, they're lying. It's not true. I force myself to take one step, then another. I need to keep moving. I spot the bathroom out of the corner of my eye, and I make a dash for it. I have to get away from the noise.`

Locking myself inside a stall, I put my hands over my ears. It's much quieter here, and the pressure in my head fades away. I take a few deep breaths. It's been months since the echoes have affected me this much. Talking to another person usually helps me tune them out, but I normally walk to class with Olive, and she's been ignoring me since our argument this morning. I hate that I have to depend on her for sanity, that by myself the slightest whisper makes me fall to pieces. I hate how weak I am.

I can't really blame Olive for being mad, though. She's been talking about senior prom for the last two years, almost the whole time we've been friends. She's convinced that it's going to be the most magical night of our lives, and she wants it to be perfect. Her echo has probably spent the whole day telling her what a bad friend I am.

Maybe I am a bad friend.

I could just come clean and explain why I don't want to go. As much as I'd like to pretend otherwise, it's not just my embarrassment of not having a date that's making me hesitate. If I can't even walk down the hallway by myself without getting overwhelmed, how am I supposed to handle prom? The echoes are going to be unbearable. If I freak out, that might ruin the night more than my absence. Surely Olive would understand.

I put my head in my hands. I can't tell her, even though I want to. How can I even begin to explain seeing echoes? I don't really know what they are, or why I'm the only one who can see them. One day I was totally normal and the next they were just there. At first, I tried to convince people not to listen to their echoes, but all it did was make them shun me. Changing schools was my saving grace, and I can't risk ruining my life again.

I wonder sometimes if I'm just crazy. Maybe it's all in my head. Logically, though, I know it's not; I've seen the way echoes impact other people. Echoes might only have negative things to say, but people listen to them without question. I can't even count the number of times I've seen a classmate's echo tell them something, and seconds later they repeat the exact same thing, or their expression changes and I can tell they heard it, too. I don't know how it works; maybe they just think they're hearing their subconscious. I wish I knew what it felt like from their side, but the only person I've never seen with an echo is me.

The bell rings, signaling that I'm late to math class. I groan. Mrs. Bradshaw isn't going to be happy with me. I leave the stall and head over to the sink. I stare at myself in the mirror as I wash the soap off my hands. There's no echo hanging over my shoulder or whispering in my ear, just the stall doors hanging open behind me.

It's a relief to hide away in my room after school. I got a lunch detention for being late to class, and Olive didn't so much as look in my direction, even when we sat right next to each other. I feel guilty, and I probably would've relented by now if it was anything else. I just can't stop imagining myself having a panic attack at prom. I can't deal with the stares, the whispers, the judgment, not again. Especially from Olive. She might be mad at me for skipping it, but she'll have Duncan and all her other friends. She won't even notice I'm gone.

My phone flashes with a text from Olive. *Please come. It won't be the same without you.* My stomach twists, and my gaze lands on the sapphire prom dress hanging in my closet. Olive forced me to go prom dress shopping with her ages ago. I'd been reluctant about the whole thing, but it was a lot of fun. We spent a whole Saturday going to different stores, trying on dresses, and laughing hysterically at the bad ones. Olive was right about shopping; maybe she'd be right about prom, too. Maybe I wouldn't fall to pieces and humiliate myself.

I look at myself in the full-length mirror hanging on my wall. Can I really do it? Am I strong enough to keep the echoes from getting to me? Can I find ways to tune them out, even when I'm alone? I'm suddenly reminded of my childhood friends, all of whom turned their backs on me the second people started calling me crazy and weird. My friendship with Olive is the only thing standing between me and the mess I used to be. I can't risk that just for a dance.

Out of the corner of my eye, I notice a shimmer in the mirror above my left shoulder. I blink a few times, but it doesn't disappear. I can't make it out. Maybe it's just some weird reflection of light.

If you go, you're going to ruin everything. The thought appears inside my brain, but I also hear it externally. It almost sounds like... I stare intently at the shimmer in the mirror, and a shape slowly fades into view. There it is. An echo. *My* echo. The one that I always thought didn't exist.

I stare at it, and it stares back at me, eyes wide. It looks exactly like me. I step back, reeling. I have an echo. It recovers from its surprise and puts on a sympathetic face. *A silly little dance isn't worth losing Olive. You're not missing anything.*

I sit down on my bed and put my head in my hands. All this time... How many lies has it told me? I always thought I could trust my inner voice, my instincts. I could see everyone else falling into the trap of their echo, but I thought I was different. Have I been listening to my echo's lies this whole time?

I think back to this morning when Olive told me about Duncan. Why did I decide not to go? Was I really embarrassed about not having a date, or was it my echo all along? What else has it ruined for me?

You should text Olive and tell her you're not going, the echo says. I can still see it in the mirror, but it isn't whispering in my ear the way echoes usually do. Instead, it makes eye contact with my reflection. I feel the urge to pull out my phone to listen to the echo. Echoes might only see the dark side of things, but that doesn't mean they're always wrong. We stare at each other for a long time, and in it, I see myself, a miserable and lonely version of myself. I don't want to become that. I've been so focused on not letting the other echoes get to me that I totally missed the way mine was controlling my life.

"I'm sorry," I tell it. I feel a strange sort of sympathy, even though I don't trust it for a second.

Its face twists in anger. *I'm trying to help you. I've only ever helped you.*

"I'm sorry," I repeat, "but I think you're wrong."

It crosses its arms and slowly fades from the reflection. Not gone, just silent.

I just stood up to an echo, I realize, and I smile. Maybe I'm strong enough after all. I pick up my phone and text Olive:

Ok.

TORMENT AT THE ASYLUM

DREW SHERMAN

CONTENT WARNINGS:
Mentions of medical neglect

Rain fell nonstop, a relentless downpour that covered everything in a gray haze. The skeletal branches of the trees surrounding the deserted asylum, resembling the bony fingers of departed souls pleading for freedom, were being hailed by the fierce wind. Samantha had always been fascinated by the old asylum. Today, as she stood in front of it, she felt a mixture of excitement and trepidation. When she was a little child, not more than four or five, her grandmother told her spooky tales about the terrible past of this asylum—a period when people with mental illnesses were formerly segregated and disregarded by society, subjected to cruel rituals conducted by bogus medical professionals to treat the terminally ill. Samantha had listened with wide-eyed wonder, her imagination weaving dark tapestries of the past. She always knew as an adult she would someday have the bravery to go investigate its secrets, tucked away behind enormous, concrete walls.

She took a deep breath and pushed open the creaking gates with an iron screech, her heart racing. The rain-soaked ground squelched beneath her boots, and the pungent scent of damp earth filled her nostrils. As she stepped further into the asylum's shadowed courtyard, she couldn't shake the feeling of being watched. Her grandmother's stories echoed in her mind, and the ancient building before her seemed to come alive with the memories of the suffering it once contained. Samantha's anxiety boiled within her, like the stormy clouds overhead, as she ventured deeper into the abyss of the asylum, her curiosity driving her forward despite the ominous aura that enveloped her. Samantha inhaled deeply and exhaled nervously. She glanced at the enormous, dilapidated building beyond, her heart pounding in her chest.

It was unknown to her that her choice would initiate a sequence of occurrences that would reveal the most sinister aspects of the asylum and reawaken the evil energies that had been dormant for an extended period. The disturbed silence that pervaded the asylum's interior was a stark contrast to the violent storm outside. Samantha's light was dull, casting feeble beams that barely pierced the oppressive darkness, revealing peeling wallpaper and crumbling walls. The sound of broken glass crunched beneath her feet as she inched further inside the decaying structure, a dissonant symphony of decay. Inside, the air was thick with the musty smell of old age and hopelessness—a stuffy mix of rotting wood, dampness, and the grief of souls that had been forgotten. The hallway opened up in front of her, the floor strewn with broken pieces of furniture, shattered remnants of an era long past, and discarded documents, some stained with mold from time's cruel hand. It felt as though the walls themselves were chatting to one another in whispers too faint for human ears, exchanging secrets that had been kept hidden for decades. Samantha couldn't escape the feeling that, by crossing this threshold, she had unwittingly opened a Pandora's box of malevolent forces that had slumbered for far too long. The unsettling sounds she had heard outside resonated inside the dark asylum, whispering. She was stuck in their mysterious embrace.

Samantha rounded a corner and found herself staring at a slightly open door. She felt as though it was calling her to explore what was on the other side. With a slow, creaking sound that sent shivers down her spine, she pushed it open. As she approached it, her heart beat out of her chest. The room was tiny, just big enough to fit a rusty metal chair and a single bed. Pictures of peaceful pastoral settings were painted on faded wallpaper, which was a harsh contrast to the stifling mood in the room. Samantha was drawn in, nevertheless, by a worn, leather-bound journal laying on the chair.

Samantha hesitated for a moment, her trembling hand hovering over the journal. Its pages were yellowed and brittle, as though time had woven a web of fragility around its secrets. Her curiosity was insatiable, and she couldn't resist the urge to uncover the hidden narrative within. The journal had the name "Emily" across the front, and as she turned through the pages, her heart sank with the weight of the past it held. Every word and line in Emily's writing showed how badly she had been hurt while she was in the hospital. She could almost feel Emily's ghostly ink on the paper, which was full of the feelings that had been spilled onto the paper. The journal revealed a horrifying story of pain, loneliness, and growing hopelessness, giving a clear picture of the deep sadness that had taken root inside these walls. Samantha got cold chills as she read Emily's entries. And the words seemed to seep into her very being. They were like the eerie echo of a soul in pain. The entries talked about strange things that happened, sounds that no one could explain, and meetings with dark beings that couldn't be explained logically. Samantha was losing her mind because Emily was going crazy, talking about a bad spirit she thought was still inside the asylum's walls. It looked like the room around her was closing in on her. The dim light was making the shadows darker and more evil, almost like they were real. As Samantha turned the pages, her fingers shook, and she felt a growing feeling of dread. The diary opened a door to a world of pain and fear, and as she read it, the line between reality and the supernatural became less clear, leaving her on the verge of a terrifying discovery.

Samantha was not even close to processing Emily's statements when a sharp surge of wind rocked the windows, her flashlight flickered and died. She was submerged in complete darkness, and when she sensed a cold presence getting closer—one that seemed to be coming from the shadows themselves—her breath exacerbated and chest tightened. Samantha's heartbeat pounded like a drum in the dark, abandoned asylum, drowning out the screams of the wind and the unsettling murmurs that had followed her. Fear shot through her veins as she fished around in her pockets for her phone, hoping the battery would last a while longer. She shook her hands and reached for her phone, turning on its weak flashlight. Its feeble glow barely managed to break through the suffocating darkness, throwing long, changing shadows around her that appeared to shake and twirl. Breathing in short gasps, Samantha turned and saw only the run-down room and its crumbling walls with her flashlight.

She felt more and more like she was being watched as she moved ahead. Every bone in her body was shivering, by whispers that brushed against her ears like the tiniest of sighs. She continued to feel the spectral presence, a terrible force that seemed to be closing in on her from all directions. With ideas of escaping the asylum gnawing at the limits of her awareness, Samantha's mind raced. Still, she was driven to continue by her curiosity and the journal she was holding in her shaking palm. She had to learn the truth about this castle and solve the riddles that resided inside its walls.

With caution, Samantha made her way down the dimly lit hallway, her meager phone light for guidance. The echoes of tormented souls, their voices begging for freedom from an eternity of pain, could be heard more clearly in the spoken in hush tones by the tormented souls/. Samantha noticed a swift movement, a glimpse of a shadowy figure vanishing into the asylum's depths. When she realized she wasn't alone, she gasped, and felt her heart racing. She was overcome with fear, but she knew she had to follow in order to face the evil that was waiting for her. The crumbling walls of the asylum seemed to come alive around her with every step she made, resonating with the agonized cries of the past. With her heart racing, Samantha trailed the dark figure further into the asylum, the meek flashlight on her phone straining to shine through the thick, oppressive blackness. The sounds of the muttering became more and more depressing.

The hallway took her to a room with a broken window, the glass glistening in the weak light like shards of ice. Samantha's eyes grew startled when she noticed the figure once more, morphing and evading in the corner. Its presence radiated evil, as if it pulling her closer, enveloping her in it. Gathering all the remaining bravery, Samantha walked up to the spector, her voice quivering as she said, "Who are you?" "What do you want?" The figure said nothing, it's strange and mysterious darkness, a terrifying reply.

Then it said, "You have awakened the tormented, intruder," in a voice that seemed as though it were echoing through the asylum's very foundations. "We yearn to be rescued from our never-ending suffering."

When Samantha realized how serious the issue was, her heart fell. The asylum was a jail for resentful spirits caught in a never-ending cycle of agony, not just a place to be abandoned. The evil force she had sensed was the misery of all the people who had died inside these walls, people who were looking for justice and escape.

At that pivotal moment, the room seemed to come to life, as if it were moving and twisting in the dim light. Shadows moved and shook, making strange, twisted forms that looked like they were reaching out to Samantha. It got very dark and sinister in the air, and she could feel cold fingers from things she couldn't see squeezing her like a trap.

As the crunching glass resonated even louder, Samantha knew she didn't have much time left; she had to move quickly because the ghosts were getting closer. She opened Emily's book with a shaking hand desperate to find something, anything that would appease the spirits. The thin pages muttered about the past, which now felt like a shroud around her. The last entry made her voice shake with fear and determination as she read it out loud. "Today the doctors say I'm going to be all better! They are conducting a breakthrough procedure called a lobotomy." The ghosts' cries of pain, which sounded like sad wails, started to fade as Samantha's words filled the room. Their ghostly shapes, which used to be scary and suffocating, began to fade away like smoke in the wind. Samantha could feel that they were leaving, but the sadness of their loss still hung over her like a disturbing tune. Samantha's voice was shaking and her breath was getting stuck in her throat as she spoke. There was a battle of wills going on against the evil that had been in this place for decades. It took Emily's sweet and ignorant words and her willingness to face the evil presence to start to turn the tide. As she read on, her voice became more steady, and her determination grew stronger. The evil presence, which had been so suffocating and all-encompassing, began to fade and go back into the dark where it came from. Samantha had gone into the darkest part of the hospital, faced the evil forces there, and come out on top. It was a moment of victory over the supernatural, but it changed her forever. She will always be connected to the hospital and the tortured souls that lived there.

"Thank you, intruder," the ghosts said one last time in a quiet group. "Peace has come to us from you." Their voices were a mix of thanks and relief, like a light breeze clearing away the heavy fog of pain that had been surrounding them for so long. Samantha was shocked by how important what she had done was as she stood in the room that had been the battlefield between the living and the restless dead.

The room, which had been a mess of supernatural chaos, went silent, as if it had been freed from the evil spirits it once harbored. Samantha's flashlight, which had been flickering and died in the dark, came back to life. Its beam of light showed the harsh truth about the asylum. It was an empty, falling apart building that had seen too much pain. Samantha walked back to the front door of the hospital, her tired and scared steps reverberating through the empty halls.

The storm was over outside, and the first weak rays of dawn light were just starting to show. It was the start of a new day. As Samantha stood at the doorway, she knew that the asylum's dark history would always be shrouded in shadows and secrets. It would always be a place where the wonders of the past would come back to haunt the living. Samantha couldn't help but wonder what her visit had really meant. Had she really brought peace to the restless spirits, or had she just added another sad chapter to their story? As she walked out into the quiet dawn, the questions were still there. The abandoned asylum would always be a creepy memory of the horrible crimes that happened inside its walls. It would always be a mystery that refused to go away, casting a haunting shadow over the land.

MANEATER

SOPHIA LEWIS

CONTENT WARNINGS:
Graphic depictions of violence, murder, body horror, blood

Cassie met Raymond for their first date on a Wednesday night. He showed up to the Italian restaurant eight minutes late, but made up for it with a bouquet of roses. She hated roses, but loved the way he looked at her with adoring hunger, and she smiled, knowing that when she invited him home after dinner, he'd oblige without hesitance.

They followed the hostess to a dark corner of the restaurant, lit by several dripping taper candles. He pulled out the chair for her and didn't bother with small talk while they looked over the menu.

"You're beautiful," he said after they ordered. Cassie feigned a blush. She knew she looked beautiful. Looking hot was the easiest way to get them to come home with her.

As they tore apart bread, they shared adolescent traumas. "I was popular," Cassie admitted, fidgeting with her napkin. She imagined herself as a typical mean girl depicted in Hollywood films, with long blonde hair and a posse. "I don't think any of my friends were genuine."

"I was the quarterback," Raymond said proudly.

Over their main courses, they laughed about college anecdotes. Raymond told her he'd studied sociology, so Cassie said she studied anthropology. He was a lawyer and she was a social worker. They'd both been part of Greek Life. "We have so much in common," was a common phrase shared between them. Cassie used to feel sorry for lying to the men she brought home. Now she reveled in the disguise.

They looked over the dessert menu, just to humor the waitress. Under the table, Cassie ran her foot up his leg, and he visibly shivered. She watched his Adam's apple bob as he closed the menu and asked for the check.

Cassie stared at him and pondered his significance. If this was a normal date, she supposed she'd ask for a second. It was in her power to end the night here, to part ways on the sidewalk and wait for him to ask her out again. But then she'd have to spend the rest of the night searching for someone else to bring home. Fear jolted up her spine just at the thought of returning home alone.

"Do you want to get out of here?" he asked as they exited the restaurant. Maybe he didn't even want a second date. Maybe he was fine with this being his last.

"Sure," Cassie smiled. "We can go to mine."

She led him down the street, his hand in one hand, his roses in another. A thorn was poking through the plastic binding, scratching her palm. His hand felt strong and soft, and he didn't complain that it was getting late, or that rain fell sporadically from the cloud cover. She sensed he was just happy to be around her, and then he told her so. She used to feel guilty at this part. Now, she was excited.

It wasn't long until they reached her house, a towering Victorian she could sell for millions, but was contractually and morally bound to keep. The house had been passed down from eldest daughter to eldest daughter for centuries. Her mother had died before it was her turn, and before her grandma passed as well she said. "It's yours now, Cassie. Take care of her. She is a burden and a blessing."

Cassie hadn't realized at the time that her grandma

wasn't referring to the house, but to its guest. Now that it was hers, she hated it. And she loved it. She lived most of her life in a similar duality.

They reached the house, an ancient house nestled in between two abandoned warehouses. It'd outlived the neighborhood that was built around and then forgotten. Its windows were dark, curtains drawn. Paint chipped, yard overgrown. It was like an old lady whose youthful beauty could sometimes be seen under layers of wrinkles.

Cassie led Raymond up the porch steps and undid the deadbolt. Before she opened the door, she turned to him, mouth open, an objection on her lips like a Freudian slip.

Then he kissed her, sweeping her up in his strong arms and the next thing she knew she was pressed up against the hallway wall, the sound of the front door clicking shut echoing behind her. This was her favorite part. The passion before disaster. She broke the kiss with a gasp, swallowed and said. "Would you like some coffee or tea?"

Raymond laughed, his hands against the wall on either side of her head. "Sure, Cass, I'd love some."

She took off her shoes—Louboutin's she'd found in the closet that morning—and led him through the house to the kitchen in the back. Along the way she turned on every light, illuminating the home her grandma had decorated in the seventies with as much light as the gaudy lamps would allow.

"I'm still working on making it my own." She said apologetically when they entered the pink kitchen. The pink wasn't the worst part. She rather liked it, but the red bathroom down the hall was atrocious. There was nothing relaxing about doing business surrounded by the color of blood. Where her grandma even found a red porcelain throne, Cassie didn't know.

Cassie put on the kettle and took two mugs from the cabinet. Raymond took off his coat and folded it over the

back of a dining chair. He checked his phone and left it
face down on the table. She leaned her hip against the
counter and pulled her hair over one shoulder, exposing her
neck to him.

"It's a lovely home. I'm so happy to be here," Raymond
said, looking directly at her. She waited for him to ask if
she was tired of living here all alone, if she wanted to fill it
with children, like the others before him had, but he didn't.
Instead, Raymond just walked over and kissed her again.

The kettle started wailing the moment Cassie heard
the first creak from upstairs. She took it off the stove and
listened. The house was silent. If Raymond had heard it, he
didn't let on.

They took their tea to the living room, and curled up
on the floral sofa with worn out cushions. Cassie folded her
legs under her and leaned towards Raymond. His aftershave
was strong. It would linger after he was gone. "I like you a
lot," he said.

She ran a finger along his collar.

Something thudded upstairs, and this time Raymond
heard His eyes widened with alarm. "What was that?"

Her pulse quickened. "Nothing. It's an old house. It's
always making noise." Cassie knew his presence had been
sensed. It wasn't long now, and she intended to enjoy every
last second. Spending time with Raymond was her attempt
to make her burden a blessing.

He put his hand on her thigh and leaned in.

Their tea went cold, and outside, the night grew darker.
They'd drifted off in each other's arms, clothes scattered on
the floor. "Cassie, I should go," Raymond whispered.

"I don't want to be alone," she murmured. "This house
is haunted." Those words jolted her all the way awake, and
she sat up, wiping drool from her cheek.

Raymond stood and offered a hand. "Let's go to bed

then,"

Cassie hesitated, listening for any more sounds from the house. She was silent, but in her time here, Cassie had learned to recognize her presence. She tugged on her underwear and shirt. She suddenly felt very cold. There was no avoiding what would happen next, no matter how hard it was to hear.

Cassie picked up their cold mugs and headed to the kitchen. "My room is on the third floor," she said over her shoulder, not daring another look at him. "I'll be up in a minute."

She heard Raymond ascending the stairs and poured the tea down the sink. She began washing the mugs, lathering the dish soap far more than she needed to. The sound of the faucet almost drowned out his first scream. Almost.

Cassie had been indignant to the houseguest when she first moved in, despite the constant echo of her grandmother's last words. "She'll need to be fed every month. She prefers men, but she'll eat either way. Don't let it be you."

The houseguest had seemed to welcome her, staying silent and surprising her with little gifts. The diamond earring she lost showed up on her nightstand, an extra twenty dollar bill in her purse. One day, the mood changed. Instead of waking up to a new outfit or spare change, Cassie's legs were bruised black and blue. The next morning, she started losing her hair. Soon after, she developed pustules and boils. That's when she knew she was hungry.

Cassie went onto a dating site and invited over the most repulsive man she could find. She didn't even touch him before directing him upstairs. The houseguest took care of the rest. The next day, the blessings started again. Thus started a perpetual cycle. Cassie felt she had lost herself somewhere along the way.

The house didn't have a third floor, but the attic stairs were right next to the second-floor stairs, narrow but hard to miss. Deceiving. There was substantial distance between the attic and the kitchen, but she could still hear the thudding and screaming.

She took an opened bottle of rosé from the fridge, sat on the floor, and waited for it to be over. She used to try to block it out completely, but now she reveled in it. She'd had fun with Raymond, she really had, and now the houseguest got her pleasure too, and tomorrow, everyone would be happy again. She was just trying to keep everyone happy.

Men shouldn't scream, she thought. They spent so much time practicing stoicism that when they finally had to scream, it sounded primal and infant-like at the same time. It was almost comedic. Almost.

Cassie tensed, however, when she heard something she wasn't supposed to hear. Footsteps coming down the stairs. She jumped to her feet as Raymond ran into the kitchen. He was still naked and now covered in blood, eyes wild like a madman. He bled from several lacerations across his abdomen. A chunk of flesh had been torn out of his shoulder, and blood slid down his arm and onto the pink tiles.

"There's a—there's a—" he gasped. "Run!"

Cassie froze. This man was bleeding out, and he'd come back for her. He cared about her. He wanted to protect her. But where was *she*? How had she let him escape? Cassie looked anxiously over his shoulder, expecting to see what she'd hoped to never witness. But the hallway was empty.

"Fuck," Cassie muttered. What was she supposed to do with this? This transaction was usually so seamless.

They both looked at his phone on the table at the same time. Raymond lurched forward, but Cassie reached it first.

Raymond fell to his knees and made a horrible drowning sound. She clutched the device but didn't make a move to dial. He gave her a pleading look, unable to speak. He needed help. Cassie dropped the phone into the sink and watched in horror and disgust, and Raymond convulsed once, twice, then went still.

The house went completely silent. Cassie poked him with her toe. She'd never felt a dead body before, so she couldn't be sure, but he didn't feel alive.

"Hello?" she called into the hallway. "He's down here. Come and get him!" Her voice cracked. Dead men in her pretty pink kitchen weren't what she signed up for.

When no reply came, Cassie swore again and rolled up her sleeves. She grabbed Raymond's ankles and dragged him down the hallway. Disregarding all the normal terrible feelings that accompanied having a man die in one's kitchen, Cassie was terrified to find out what would happen if her houseguest wasn't fed.

Raymond was already dead, so there was no use risking her own life as well.

Gritting her teeth, she tugged his body up the stairs, heaving him up one step at a time. When she finally reached the top, she paused to catch her breath, eying the attic staircase warily. For a moment, she hated the houseguest more than she feared her. This level of service was ridiculous. But still, she ascended to the attic.

Cassie dragged Raymond's body into the center of the floor and retreated to the top of the stairs. It was silent, and the light switch still didn't work. She peered into the space, the boxes, and old furniture slightly illuminated by the streetlights outside. It smelled like decay and rust. It felt like a furnace.

Across the room, something moved. She jolted violently, heaving a silent sigh when she realized it was just her own reflection in a large, cracked mirror. Hair askew, blood on her hands and feet, she looked like the ghost of a murder victim hovering at the top of the stairs.

"You are a guest in my house," she said. A lump formed in her throat.

A pair of eyes blinked at her from the corner. Cassie fought the urge to run.

"You," the voice reverberated, mirroring her own.

Cassie pointed at Raymond, willing her voice not to waver. "You let him escape. Don't let it happen again."

They were both silent, the glinting eyes disappeared. Cassie lifted her chin and descended the stairs. She could pretend all she wanted that this was her house, but deep down she knew that she was the houseguest.

HOW TO GET OVER YOUR STUPID EX

CHEYENNE GARDNER

CONTENT WARNINGS:
Depression

I remember so distinctly the sweet smell of the ink and paper in my book. The quiet hum of the lights that flickered softly. I remember how the pages in my book had scales—tiny, fuzzy dents and little marks on the paper. I remember the golden lamps and the creaky leather chair that wrapped me in its teal blue arms, like a tender hug that encompassed my entire body.

I started reminiscing about our relationship. How in each delicate page I saw a romance I thought I could only dream of. I paid attention to how your voice reminded me of the flickering lights and how the pages of the book reminded me of the soft cotton clothes you would wear. When this thought of mine continues, I am reminded of that lovely teal chair. The one I loved so greatly. The one I would do absolutely anything for. The smooth leather protected itself from most tears and drink spillings.

Soon enough, you reminded me too much of that chair. The arms wrapped themselves around my chest, hands, and throat despite my trying to motion for you to stop. The teal leather slowly suffocated me. My fear of you leaving consumed me, and I felt like I couldn't take a breath of air. It was real. I slept for months after you left. My process was simple. Sleep, wake up, take meds, sleep. I was awake for no more than five minutes; my body was too weak from not eating, and that was how long it took for the sleeping pills to have their effect. When you left, I still felt haunted by you. I searched the internet for articles on how to get rid of you and the feelings you had left me with.

Eventually, I found something that I thought could help me. A WikiHow article: How to Get Rid of a Ghost in Your House (& Signs Your House is Haunted).

1. Cleanse your house.

Open your windows to let in some fresh air and sunlight, and burn lavender or sage incense to infuse your home with a fresh, lively scent. Deep-cleaning your house can exorcise any paranormal energies lurking there.

- A clean, fresh-smelling house is also a major mood booster, and our own positive vibes may help eliminate any negative ones.
- Light white candles anywhere you've sensed paranormal activity: this will help fight any negative energies as well.

I stopped there on the page. Why would I open the window when the sunlight reminded me of you? The lavender reminded me of the lotion we bought together, the same one I would fall asleep with you rubbing on my shoulders. I didn't have the motivation to do anything the article told me anyway.

2. Protect your space.

Once you've banished your ghost and cleansed your home of any negative vibes, it's important to set up spiritual barriers to prevent any new paranormal entities from entering. You can protect your space with specific stones—but if you've got to order them online, you can get a jumpstart on shielding your house using plain old table salt.

- Create a ring of salt around your house to protect it from spirits entering. Any spirit, good or...not good, who wants to enter your house will be unable to cross the salt barrier.
- Set howlite and tourmaline around your house to protect you from negative spiritual energy. Putting agate by your bedside may help you have sweeter dreams.

I closed my computer, and it stopped whirring after a brief moment. I tapped my fingers gingerly against my desk and let out a big sigh. I didn't feel like exorcizing you, and I did not want to sprinkle any salt. I reminisce on how I shook too much over your sandwich. The grains were invisible, but you quickly swooped in and scraped the sauce covered in salt with a butter knife. Your friend wagered a crinkly twenty-dollar bill if you licked the Dijon mustard that must've held a good percentage of the ocean's salt content. Two minutes later, there was a burst of laughter and coughing, followed by the sink water running. I replayed the video your friend took over and over and fell further into my cycle of sleep, wake up, take meds, and sleep. A thousand plays later, I decided to put up rings of salt. Nothing changed. I had sweet dreams, but that's why I slept. The dreams would be of us together.

My cycle was soon disrupted by my friends and therapist reaching out to check on me. They bore witness to the catastrophic events I managed to survive through. I ghosted them a month after the worst went down. I felt tired, but I found defeat in the way I was feeling. I felt lonely and needed to surround myself with warmth and welcomeness. It still couldn't compare to yours, but it was a start. The following weeks filled themselves as I chatted briefly with friends and went to therapy, where I would cry through my rage, fondness, and sadness.

After going through a few thousand boxes of tissues covered in mascara and tears, I bought some rocks and placed them around my bed, on the shelf, and next to my romance books. Nothing changed. The dreams would continue to be of us together.

My life was this endless loop for a while, and I was careful not to alter my grieving process. I was hesitant as I could feel my memories of us changing. I will not forget you. I will not get over you. I know it is meant to be, and it will be. That mindset stuck with me for weeks. I found hope in watching your playlist being looped on the regular. For every romance song you played, it was like a petal ripped from a delicate flower saying, "he likes me."

Eventually, I found myself drowning in flower petals. Some wilting from the angry breakup music that you played. The flower petals smelt sickly sweet, like fruit rotting at the end of the season. Poltergeists are no joke. I needed you gone, and I needed to heal. I opened my computer back up and firmly clicked on the bookmarked page. I was prepared to move on to the next step. I wanted to; I was tired of being drowned, and I ran out of tears to cry. I knew I wouldn't be able to sleep with these emotions flooding me.

3. Tell the ghost to leave you alone.

It may sound obvious, but sometimes the most direct approach is the most helpful. Your ghost may not realize it's an unwelcome presence in your home, so telling it (politely) to leave may be effective.

- Next time you feel the ghost's presence, say something like, "Please leave." If your ghost is

really bugging you, be a bit more forceful: "You're
not welcome here. I command you to go."

You were a welcome presence. You are welcome
here. I command you to stay. Please. I was folded over my
computer. Tears wet the keys that weren't covered by my
fingertips. Hours lasted like this. No appetite, no will. There
was nowhere else I thought I would need to be. None of
it mattered because I didn't matter without you. Nothing
mattered if I didn't have you. I thought I was ready to heal
and move on, but tears continued streaming down my
face. I stood from my chair, trembling, and crumpled into
the heap of clean laundry sitting on my bed. I wrapped
myself in whatever warm fabric came to my fingertips
first. Eventually, I had a mountain of laundry, pillows, and
blankets nesting me. I slept in that spot for weeks like
that. When I was awake for too long my thoughts would
spiral into a demonic entity that screamed the story of you
leaving me. I was hopeless each time I wouldn't wake to
a notification from you. Not even the funniest jokes could
make me crack a smile.

I jolted awake one night, a shiver running down my
spine. I gripped my phone off the charging cord and turned
it on. I stared at the glaring numbers on my phone. It was
three in the morning. I got up for the first time in weeks
and sat at the end of my bed. The thoughts loomed over
me, and I contemplated them. I was alone, isolated, and I
called a hotline.

I was scared of who I had become. I was wheeled
off to the hospital that day and kept in an eerie room. My
clothes and belongings were taken and held hostage, I was
forced to wear an uncomfortable teal outfit made of a rough
cotton that felt similar to cardboard. It was nothing like
the chair or your clothes. My stay could not replace what I
missed about you, so why was I here? Surely, these doctors

couldn't fix what I had lost. I sat in the pale blue and white room with lights that made me think of a horror movie. All I had were my thoughts and some crackers. I cried, and the nurse wrapped me in a heated blanket as I curled into the cemented square that had a flat mattress glued to it. I was traumatized.

The doctors had provided me with some socialization but ultimately could not fix what I was left with. They pushed me further into frequent therapy sessions, a couple of hours every week. My therapist urged me to interact with the world around me, to find something to fill the void I felt while challenging my tendencies for codependency. After a session, I sat down outside and opened up the app store on my phone. I downloaded a few dating apps and some apps to meet people. Their logos slowly popped up on my screen, and I started typing in my basic information. I finished creating my profile and started swiping. I then began chatting with a couple of people. A few questionable dates and awkward car rides later, I returned to my desk. None of them were you. I was trying to move on, but you haunted me. I opened my computer and clicked around until I reopened the page one last time.

4. Ignore them.

Some ghosts just want attention (don't we all?). If you tend to react to creaking floorboards or unexplained whispers with, "Who's there?" your ghost may feel encouraged to continue their behavior. Pretending it doesn't bother you may send the message to your ghost that they should give it up.

- Even if you're terrified of ghosts, "faking it 'til you make it" may help you become less afraid of your ghost over time.

Ignore them. The words burnt into my retinas as the

fan of my computer hummed. I ignored you for months after that. Sometimes I thought about saying something but decided against it. I ignored you, and I am thankful. I watched as your ghost went away and my eyes stopped filling with clouds.

Sometimes, I'm still haunted by you. I think of the things you put me through. I will not forgive, and in some ways I have. I am in conflict with my emotions and self-interest, but I find myself easing back into the teal blue chair. My fingers trail the spine of the book, cracked and peeling. The pages have scales and dents. The lights still hum quietly, and they flicker as well. I no longer feel bound to you or stuck in the creases of the leather. I envelop myself in a romance book that I end up enjoying because I am no longer haunted by your ghost, the love that couldn't begin to compare to what is written on these pages.

THE MAN AND THE HOUSE

DAWSON HOSE'

"Why haven't you left yet?'

I've wanted to leave you,
Forget you,
Move on from you,

Remove the numbness that you left inside of me,
Eating away from me slowly,
Like a parasite taking over control of my body.

Slowly losing who I once was,
Losing the best parts of me.
I tried not to think about it,
Not give it a single thought.

I peek at the mirror,
To see myself.
My reflection is the same,
But at the same time
Completely different.
I don't recognize myself,
Who this new man in the mirror was.

Yet,
I choose to stay in this house,
This house that we built.

I tried to leave,
Made it a mile away.

But that was as far as I could go.
Every step I took haunted me,
Cause I knew leaving
Would hurt worse than a parasite.

So I stay here,
In this haunted house,
Of our past
And the future we could have had.

I'd rather be here,
And stay cursed by what could have been,
Then leave,
And be torn apart with regret.

BLOOD IN THE SNOW

THOMAS ALEJANDRO

CONTENT WARNINGS:
Blood, murder, violence

Have you ever done one of those assignments from your teacher asking where you'll be X years from now? Some kids answer that they'll be a famous artist or running their family business. Other kids give a more serious answer saying that they are going to be spending the rest of their lives making ends meet. Now normally you'd say surviving would be an exaggeration, but in my case, it's more on point, especially when you're trapped somewhere with a killer nearby.

It may sound like I'm getting ahead of myself but I've been questioning since that night, why me? All I wanted was to make a nice warm dinner for everyone who stayed behind. The school we lived at had made an offer for those that stayed behind during the holiday break to look after the campus and would find that there would be a little less they owed Though it meant not spending Christmas with my family, it was a decision that was better for the future so that we would all have a less financially stressful future. Some students and I students stayed behind, and as such, all we had for the holidays were each other.

As I was walking back, almost near the campus I call home away from home, I lost my footing on the icy sidewalk and fell to the floor. After cursing the cold under my breath,

I saw blood in the snow beneath. I began to check myself for any cuts or injuries, but I seemed okay. I looked back down at the snow, and against my better judgment, I followed the blood. When it became more of a puddle, I dug with my gloved hands, protected from the cold yet stained in dark red, until I saw something that would forever haunt most people. It was fingers. They weren't a normal skin color as they had turned blue and at first glance, you could mistake them for icicles that hang from the bottom of a roof. I then heard a voice call out, asking if I was ok. For a moment, I froze before I yelled back, "CALL THE POLICE. I FOUND SOMEONE, AND HE'S DEAD!"

So much happens that when I finally regain focus, I find myself in a room with just a door, and I have no idea how long it's been. The door to my left opens, and in walks a man, mid-30s, who isn't wearing a cop's uniform, so he is most likely a detective. He sits down and gently places a folder on the desk. "Hi, Oswald," he says. "Can I call you Oswald?"

"That is my name, but people call me Oz."

"Like the wizard?" he asks. Figures. Most people older than me ask that.

"Not exactly."

He gives a hint of a smirk. "My name is Detective Will Stevens, and I've been assigned to the case you just made."

"By finding the body?"

"Yes. I know that the past couple of hours have been a lot, but it's important that you tell me everything you know so we can find out what happened. Looking at what you told the officer on the scene, you were walking back to your school campus from the store when you tripped, noticed some blood in the snow, and dug up a body. When a pedestrian saw you, you yelled at them to call the Police. Is there anything else?"

"Yeah, I knew him. Cole Brentman. He was staying with

us over the holidays, but he disappeared. We thought he changed his mind and left."

He looked at me, waiting for me to continue. "I'm going to need some more information."

"The School is doing a trial program. Some students stay behind for the holidays, cleaning, maybe some maintenance, and a few walks around the campus each day so no one does something stupid like break in. In exchange, part of our tuition is paid off."

"And you two are a couple of these students? How many of there are you in total?

"Eight. Me, Cole, and six others," I yawn.

"Alright, I think that's enough for tonight. I'll have an officer drive you home, and in the morning, we'll be at the campus, where we'll need to question everyone there." He thanks me and walks me out, where an officer is right there. He opens the door to the back of the car and I get in. He closes the door, gets in the car, and starts the engine. To the side, I see groceries, and I don't need to look inside to know that the food has started to go bad.

I can barely wake up when I hear the knock at the door and Sean saying, "Hey Oz, you better get downstairs. The police are here." I'm one step ahead of him because I'm still in the same clothes from last night, though my lack of energy didn't stop my brain from spinning about everything that happened last night.

I head downstairs, and I see the six other students here, Detective Stevens, along with what looks like his partner, A woman, I'm guessing mid-20. There are also two other officers here, and Stevens addresses us.

"Good morning. Last night, the body of one of your classmates was discovered, Mr. Cole Brentman." He pauses as he lets it sink in for everyone. "I know this comes as a shock, but trust me, we are going to do everything we can to catch his killer. That means my partner, Detective

Runes, and I will need to ask you all some questions."
The detectives take a room, each pulling someone in for
questioning. The other two officers stay to watch us. When
my turn comes, I'm back face to face with Stevens.

"I take it by the looks of shock you didn't tell anyone
about this." I stay quiet. "We've informed Cole's family.
They are flying in today to claim his body." No comment.
"Is there anything else you can remember, something you
might have forgotten to tell me last night?"

"Do you think one of us killed him?"

He doesn't answer for a moment. "We are looking into
every possibility there is."

After the police leave, everyone starts talking. I look at
them, thinking one of them could be the killer. Six possible
people who could have taken Cole's life. Knowing their
names was something that sent a shiver down my spine, the
fact that I may know a killer. Jasmine, Lucas, Sean, Riley,
Max, and Felipe. I keep my distance, but not for long, as
Sean approaches me.

"Why are you off on your own?" he asks.

I hesitate. "I've never been good at conversations.
What am I supposed to say?"

"I don't know, something comforting?"

"Comfort? Who here really knew Cole?"

"You'd be surprised."

I hardly sleep that night. Who else here wants to be
near a potential killer? You'd be surprised. What did Sean
mean by that? I can't stop thinking about it. I knock on his
door, and a moment later, he opens it. "What is it?" he asks,
yawning. I'm surprised he can even get a wink of sleep.

"What did you mean by 'you'd be surprised?'" He takes
his time getting an answer out, like he's using being tired
as a defense.

"Everyone here knew Cole, except for you I guess."

True, I'm not the most socially active. "Everyone here

knew him?"

"Yeah." Possible motivation. "Look, I'm tired. It's been a long day, and I could use some sleep."

The next day, I walk outside, needing the fresh air. As I go out to the road, I see a couple standing at the place where I found Cole. I walk over and ask if they're his parents. I could tell they were related by the tears running down their face and falling to the ground before they could be turned into ice.

"Yes, we are," says the father. "You knew him?"

I answer honestly, "No, I didn't know him." I debated for a moment before going on. "I found him here." They both look at me, but I don't know what they are thinking. I know it's something they deserve to know, but should they already be hurting more than they are? I'm surprised when the mother hugs me.

I can hear the pain in her voice. "Thank you for finding him." She then let me go. "I know Christmas is only five days away, and it's going to be painful, but something tells me it would be a lot worse worrying about him for longer."

I try to think of something comforting to say, but I can't. "Do the police have any leads?"

The father answers, "They are short-handed, most of 'em spending this time with their families. I don't blame them, but I hope that this doesn't give the person who did this to our boy the chance of evading punishment."

"I'm sorry that your son was taken from you. I hope that whoever did this will face justice."

The mother looks at me, holding back tears. "I don't know if they ever will, but I do hope so."

I don't know why it had to be me that found Cole like that, but now I can't get his face out of my head. It disturbed me, his appearance slowly becoming the color of snow, the blood freezing up to look like it was frosting on his skin, the lack of life in his eyes. It seems as if the blood was mainly on the right side. The weapon couldn't have been a gun, there's no way someone could sneak one on campus. Not to mention, there were no gunshot wounds.

The last time I had seen Cole was dinner time. We had all gathered to eat dinner because there was a deal for a family feast. Everyone was all social and interactive, making the best out of the situation we were in. Everyone was having a good time with each other, except for me. Cole then left, the look on his face unpleasant, like it was something he wasn't looking forward to. Maybe a confrontation with the person who ended up killing him. He left, and then he died.

Ok, I have the time of death. Now is the who. Sean said everyone knew him, so I scoured the internet and social media, collaborations of their relationships and activities, and I saw the big picture.

The next morning, I rushed over to the police station, and I remembered what Cole's parents had said about the lack of police. There was one desk sergeant and a couple of officers. I knew Stevens was here because this case is open. We met in the interrogation room, and he asked if I remembered anything else to help.

"No, but I've learned some stuff about my classmates, and they all had a connection to Cole." He looks at me, trying to figure out where I'm going. "I spent all of last night looking through theirs and Cole's social media. Cole was one of the stars of the Football team, and Sean was another, though less popular. It also seems like Cole had a lot of the spotlight on the Football team that Sean might have been jealous of."

"Okay, son, that's something, but I wouldn't say that makes a motive or anything."

"That's not all," I continued. He's made a few enemies. He likes making fun of some of the transfer students, especially Felipe, even going so far as to make some cruel pranks. It also looks like he broke up with his girlfriend, Riley, because they haven't been in each other's posts since the end of October. She even went so far as to post things about self-healing. Then there's a weird triangle between Jasmine, Lucas, and Max. Lucas and Cole nearly got into a fight at the Thanksgiving game. Lucas and Max are a couple, and Max and Jasmine are friends. They all have something in common, and that something was something against Cole."

Stevens processes all this, but he doesn't give the response I expect. "I can see you put time into this, but I don't think any of this can lead to one of them killing." I thought this was what he wanted. They thought one of us was the killer, and I know it's not me. Just the idea of a killer being nearby sends a chill down my body.

"I know you want to help, but this doesn't provide any solid evidence, motive, or opportunity. There is nothing here I can go off of."

His words stuck in my brain as I tried to physically piece this together. When I return to my room, I scribble and tear out the pages of my notebook, stick them to the wall, and connect everything with tape. I'm just trying to figure out what happened and bring myself peace. I must have been alone in my thoughts for hours because the commotion in my head stops from a knock on the door.

"Oswald," Max says. "We are having a group dinner meeting downstairs, and we want you to join us." I walk down and see the others gathered around, waiting for me. Joining the group, Felipe starts the meeting.

"We've been talking, and we think it best to stick together. We shouldn't be alone."

I know they mean well, but who can I trust? One of them has to be Cole's killer. I respond politely, "I understand and appreciate the thought, but right now, I feel best being on my own."

Lucas fires back, "Someone died! Do you really think any one of us should be alone?"

I can't control myself. "Do you know what it's like to dig up a frozen and bloodied body? What's it like to see that every time you're alone? To ask yourself why it had to be me? Huh?" No one says anything, and I get up to leave.

"We're not done here!" I hear Lucas following me to my room, and I try to get in and close the door, but he barges in, and all I hear is, "What the actual fu-"

Suddenly, everyone is looking at the wall I had made, where they were all suspects in Cole's Murder. In their shock, I bolted past them and ran from my room. I knew this would make me look guilty, but I couldn't have handled their reactions. I hid for the rest of the day, and on my way to a new spot, I ran right into Sean.

"Sean, listen, I know it looks bad, but I had to figure out who killed Cole. "

"And I guess everyone was fair game on the board."

"You all had something against Cole, a motive, and being here isolated from others gave you opportunity."

"So, what was my motive for killing Cole?"

I debate momentarily, but he'll tell others where I am, so I spill. "You were one of the best players on the Football Team. You were even meant to be scouted out, but Cole took your spotlight."

Sean smirks and chuckles. "He shouldn't have even been on the team for that long. He was doing so badly in his classes that he should have been kicked off the team. But he somehow stayed on. I didn't take it too personally, especially after hearing that it caused him and Riley to break up."

Now that's something new. I have to dig deeper. "What do you mean?"

"I heard that he got a tutor. Someone that Riley didn't end up liking in the end. The two got into a big fight before the Halloween party, and they broke up then and there."

This is mind-blowing. I thank Sean and run back to my room. I tear down Sean's page, and I think. Riley was angry at Cole, so that still makes her a suspect. I tear down Filepe's page. There was no way Felipe would tutor Cole after the prank. Lucas, Max, and Jasmine are also here, but I can't seem to figure out which one is connected the most to Cole. Then, I have an idea of who it might be. I arm myself with a letter opener in one hand and my phone's flashlight in the other and walk out.

"AAAAAAAAAAAHHHHHHH!" I hear a scream, and I run towards it, and when I get to the source, I....

I...

I can't believe it. On the floor is Sean's body. The blood is fresh, staining his gray shirt and sports coat. The carpet transitions from a dark blue to purple-violet. He still has some life in him, and Lucas asks, "What happened? Who did this?"

Sean sees me in his side view and uses all the life he has left to turn to face me. "Oz, you... You have..." he mutters as his breathing stops and his eyes freeze. Both Max and Lucas look at me as Felipe arrives.

"MURDER!" Max cries out. Felipe pulls out his phone, and I know he's calling 9-1-1.

"If you know what's good for you, put down the knife and don't move," Lucas demands. "The police are on their way, and you are going away for the rest of your life."

I'm not the killer. I didn't kill Sean. I didn't kill Cole. But they won't believe me. They're scared, and so am I, but I have everything to lose if I don't figure it out. So I run. I run to the stairwell and I can hear Lucas running behind me, yelling for me to stop. I hear him picking up speed, so I rip a fire extinguisher off the wall and chuck it down the stairs.

Lucas swears in pain as the canister collides with him.

I reach the fourth floor and just keep running. I race down the hallway, and I can hear from the volume of Lucas' voice that he's picking up speed and almost caught up. I race around the corner, and I'm suddenly pulled into a room. It's Jasmine, and she puts her hands out to calm me down.

"It's okay. Breathe," she says.

I catch my breath, and as soon as I do so, I ask why she's helping me.

"'C'mon, there's no way you could have killed Cole."

That intrigues me, and a light pops into my head. "Would you feel safer if I handed you the knife?"

"That would make me feel more safe," She responds. "And you can also turn your flashlight off, it's beaming directly into my eyes."

I do turn my flashlight off, but not before starting a recording. I then hand her the letter opener, and she grabs it with her left hand. I placed the phone back in my pocket before asking, "What do you mean that there was no way I could have killed Cole?"

"Because Cole can put up a fight when he wants to. Believe me, I know."

"I'm having a hard time believing that."

"Cole and I sat next to each other for class this fall. I couldn't believe it, the most popular guy on the football team sat right next to me. I was crushing so hard. But I also knew I was way out of his league, so I thought nothing of it."

"I'm still lost here. How do I believe you know Cole?" I have to confirm this.

"Well, an opportunity struck as rare as lightning to a person. One day, when I was leaving class, I heard him begging the professor, saying he couldn't fail this class or he'd get kicked off the team. The professor couldn't do anything, but I could. I offered to tutor him. He accepted, and I helped him out with his homework. But a big exam was coming up, and he wasn't ready. So he asked me to help him cheat. And told him I had to be crazy to help him cheat."

"Did you?"

"For something in return. The night before the exam, he came over for a late-night study session, and what he paid was incredible. That's how I know he can put up a fight when he wants to."

Almost. "But didn't he have a girlfriend?"

"Oh yeah, I thought she and him had a rough patch and that they were done. I believed that our time was about to blossom. But when I found out he wanted to end what we had to heal things up with her, I lost my mind."

"And so you killed him." She looks at me, and the face of shock tells me everything. I go on. "Sean told me Cole got a tutor, and that played into him and Riley breaking up. So when Cole ended things with you, you got Max and Lucas involved. Maybe you thought the pressure would make him reconsider, but it also meant you weren't the prime suspect."

Jasmine processes everything, then asks, "And you got all that from my story?"

"Nope." I replied. "You grabbed the knife with your left hand. Cole was stabbed in the right side of his body. You telling me allowed me to answer the motive, and this little school trial gave you the opportunity when there were other people who didn't like Cole. And when I became the most suspicious, you killed Sean so that I would take the fall." I pulled out my phone and stopped the recording. "You're going to end up far worse than expelled, Jasmine."

She chuckles. "That's pretty good detective work. But aren't you forgetting something?" She holds the letter opener tightly in her left hand. "I am sorry you found the body, but if you would have let this go, you may have survived this winter."

I heard Stevens yelling, looking to take me in.

"OZ! THIS IS DETECTIVE STEVENS! GIVE UP NOW! WHERE ARE YOU?!"

I seize my moment. "IN HERE DETEC-"

I'm interrupted by Jasmine's scream as she charges at me with the knife. I barely dodge, and I quickly replay the recording on high volume. Jasmine continues to swipe at me as I go to unlock the door. I turn the knob, but Jasmine gets my shoulder. I cry out in agony, hoping for Stevens to arrive. She pins me to the floor and holds the knife over my head.

"TIME FOR YOU TO SHUT UP!" Jasmine yells. As I prepare to see the light, the door bursts open, and I can hear the sweet sound of Steven's voice.

"JASMINE HEARD, YOU ARE UNDER ARREST FOR THE MURDER OF COLE BRENTMAN! PUT THE KNIFE DOWN NOW!" I feel relief for a moment, but the pain overtakes me, and the world goes black.

I wake up slowly, wondering if it had all been a dream, until I hear a familiar voice. "Oh, thank goodness you're awake." I turn to my right, and I see Felipe, Max, Lucas, and Riley all next to me. It hits me that I'm in the hospital. "We owe you an apology for everything that happened last night. You saved us."

I'm still coming to when Riley starts to explain everything. "That cop showed up when we called about you. He went looking and found you at Jasmine's mercy. You found out what she did and risked your life to reveal the truth. He arrested her, called in paramedics, and brought you here. We came along after." Stevens walks in at that moment.

"Well I'm glad you're doing alright. Doctor says you can be out by this evening, so you won't spend the holiday in a hospital."

"Well, ain't that a Christmas miracle," I reply. It got a laugh out of everyone, even Riley.

"Would you all give us a moment?" Stevens asks. They all nod and leave the room, and Stevens closes the door behind them. "I gotta be honest, I wouldn't have thought that this girl was our killer. You did well, Sherlock."

"Thanks, but I just wanted this nightmare to be over."

I was released from the Hospital late on Christmas Eve. When I was discharged, I called my parents and assured them I would be okay. We spent the remainder of the time together, healing and forming bonds I thought had been long broken. The school put the trial on hold so they could legally prepare themselves. And when the next term began, I was the most popular kid on campus. I got all kinds of interview requests and was lucky if I could eat one meal in peace. But what got me the most was as the winter was ending, I somehow returned to the spot where I found Cole. I looked down below at my hand, and I still saw the barely visible bloodstain, though looking back up, I could see Cole, and now Sean as well, both looking more human as all the blood on their bodies disappeared. They gave me a little smile before fading away. I know I will never be able to forget what happened, but I can at least rest knowing we are all at peace.

THE DOG

KAYLA PASKEWICH

CONTENT WARNINGS:

Graphic depictions of abuse, graphic depictions of violence, blood

The Man's Best Friend

The Dog is a loyal animal. It is skinny, with a spine that peeks out It's back like jagged, worn, mountains, and a wide, bony rib cage. It walks with a slow, almost limp-like gait. The Dog's eyes have a sad, half-closed look to them. When the Dog looks at anyone, It has an intense and pained expression, with lips drawn tight and eyebrows furrowed. This all changes when Its Master is near, for which, the Dog is rarely without.

It has many names, too many for It to even remember, but mostly just "the Dog". These words are used frequently when the Master speaks about the Dog to other people.

It's necessary for a Dog's livelihood to have mankind, and It is lucky to even have one man in It's life. Without Its Master, the Dog is nothing but wild and can be a terrifying sight. When the Master is home with His Dog, the Dog follows Him everywhere. To the kitchen, around the bedroom, all throughout the house, anywhere, the Dog will follow the Master around, mouth wide and tail wagging. If the Master decides to settle down, the Dog will lay by His side, but not too close.

Once, the Dog settled very close, as It did when the Master first got It. The Master, who had a long day at work, smacked It across Its muzzle and It yelped for the first time in pure agony. The Dog was so frightened it ran right out an open window. It came back shortly, and the Master berated It. It never ran away again after that.

The Dog meant nothing by it, It just wanted to be pet and held like most Dogs do.

When the Master is away, the Dog stays in the Yard. A tired, rusty dark chain-link fence surrounds the Yard, with dry, dead grass that fills the expanse. A singular old dog toy sits in the grass, having been shredded beyond recognition over the years. If anyone walks by the fence, the Dog will not go near, not even to investigate. If the Dog is called over, It will bark and snap at anyone who dares to approach, which the Master taught It to do. It was a good Dog. Some feel sorry for the Dog, some are disgusted because of Its unruly, isolating behavior. What Dog doesn't want to be around people? But this Dog only has loyalty for one in Its heart. Is that bond something one can break?

The Eyes

One day, something different happened. Most days for the Dog are spent in the Yard while the Master is away. It was a rather monotonous schedule for the Dog. This day was unusual. The Dog saw another shape walking outside of the fence, but it wasn't human. The Dog felt the hairs on the back of Its neck begin to stand straight up in fear, the animal had no smell. It didn't even know why It was so scared. The animal had a powerful aura to it. The Dog approaches cautiously, curiosity overtaking. The shape of another dog appeared in Its vision as It peered through the fence. She stood tall despite not being the largest dog, and

Her eyes were bright with youthful energy. The Dog noticed though, that there was no other human leading Her around, no collar around Her neck either. She looked like the Dog, but She was lean and strong yet covered in old scars, like It. A similar breed, maybe. But there was no way She could be It, no matter how similar and uncanny their resemblance. This dog was wild and It was not.

She wagged her tail in a friendly way, and the Dog was surprised to find Itself approaching close to where She was. At first, when the other dog reached to sniff Its face through the small rusty, black diamonds of the chain-link fence, It flinched. However She waited, tail wagging low and patiently, so It let Her take in the information She needed. The Dog wanted to recoil away as soon as the other dog pressed Her snout against Its own, but something held It still. She also stays still, as if to say *"I know you, I've been you. I know what you've been through, and I'm sorry."* It found Itself lying on the ground, with a large sigh. The other dog watched It, warm brown eyes brimming with sympathy and sadness. The Dog looked back up, watching the other dog turn around, Her tail like a sickle in the air. She looked back at It, a different expression of determination on Her face. It knew what She was trying to say: *"I'll come back for you when you're ready."* The Dog glances back toward the House, feeling unsure. *When I'm ready? What would she mean by that?*

But when It turned back, She was gone.

I could never be wild, the Dog tried to tell Itself with decidedness.

The Head

When the Master returned that night, the Dog was excited, but less so than usual. After greeting the Master, the Dog settled down on the kitchen floor, curling up tightly into a ball and sighing with a deep exhale. Its mind was very troubled. It felt like rabbits were running around in circles in Its brain.

"What's wrong?" The Master rumbled.

The Dog's heart nearly jumped out of Its chest when the Master placed His hand on Its head, but not in a threatening way. A distant memory came to Its mind; them staring into each other's eyes, music, dancing, they were happy once. Its heart ached as It thought, *it isn't like that anymore, is it?*

It hadn't even realized that The Master was speaking to It, let alone starting to get loud, and clearly frustrated. The Dog was so absorbed in Its memories, the feelings of joy and newness, when the Master first took It home and gave It a shiny new collar, something It had never had before. That memory was broken as It felt a sharp, precise slap across the nose. It stumbled, finding Itself staring at the floor, feeling dazed and shocked. It didn't want to meet eyes with the Master anymore.

It found Itself having to hold Its mouth closed, despite the stinging pain. The urge to bite was there, and that urge was much worse than it ever had been. *A bad dog bites the hand that feeds It,* It reminds Itself. *I'm not wild. I'm a good dog that stays like good dogs should.* It wasn't even as bad as it could've been. But the image of the Other Dog appeared in Its mind, an image so clear, so confident and free. No man to tie Her down and put a collar on Her. She almost didn't even seem real. Wild dogs were supposed to be skinny and sickly, as well as uncooperative and unruly. Now was the urge to run away, like It had done before, and that was even harder to fight. But It reminded Itself what makes a good dog over and over as the night went on.

The Master filled Its bowl that night, which surprised the Dog. "You don't really deserve this, but you need to eat and I love you, despite everything." He said as He walked away holding a bag of dog food. Normally, this filled the Dog with such a warmth that made It feel a strong renewed sense of devotion for this man, someone who gave It a new home and kept It fed, and at times showed a love that the Dog had never known. The Dog felt Its stomach turn to stone with the very thought of eating. *Maybe I'll try tomorrow,* It thought as It went to the small pillow that was Its bed. It curled up in a ball, and with eyes heavy, It drifted to sleep, the weariness overwhelming It even though Its mind was troubled.

The Mind

The very next day when The Master left for work, The Dog was sent to the Yard again, as It did any day that The Master went to work. It felt uneasy today, though. Before the Master had left, He patted The Dog on the head and said "Be good today."

That was unusual too, it seemed like things were more unusual for The Dog as of late, which made It feel confused and nervous. *What changed? Does he know about the Other Dog?* It considered, with a fluttery, anxious feeling in Its chest. *No, he can't. He'd be angrier if he found out I hadn't chased her away. I can't let Him find out, I'd be a bad dog.* The Dog knew what It had to do if It saw her again. At the end of the day, the Master was the most important voice in It's life. Nothing could change that.

It waited close to the fence as the sun shifted in the sky. It seemed like the world had gone still, not even a whisper passed by. The Dog started to turn back, maybe it was the case that the Other Dog wasn't real, like It had thought.

And then, she was there. The Dog stopped in Its tracks, sensing that strong presence. It spun around to face her at the fence, teeth bared and eyes wide with a vicious growl in Its voice. She stared back, unshaken. The Other Dog just cocked her head sympathetically, looking intently at It.

"I know that's not actually how you feel." She replied.

The Dog froze, and looked down at the grass beneath Its feet, feeling slightly shocked. *That's the first time she actually spoke to me.* But it doesn't matter, she needs to go. "My Master said that I can't allow anyone near me, or the fence, so leave!" It snapped.

The Other Dog's eyes softened. "I'm glad to hear your voice." She frowned though. "You sound hurt. Your Master, he doesn't treat you well, does he?" She came closer to the rusty bars, almost until their noses touched. It flinched away, closing Its eyes. "I can tell, but you're so strong. You're not just some Dog."

The Dog looked at her, confused.

"I know you better than you think. You're a being with a soul and a strong mind, I don't think your Master deserves your loyalty when you've given up so much of yourself for him," She said gazing at It.

The Dog considered this but sighed. "I can't leave Him. I love Him." The Other Dog sat herself by the fence, sighing too.

"Love shouldn't require you to lose who you are. You should know you are free at heart." Thinking deeply about this, It felt something burn in Its heart, like the blaze that sits in The Master's fireplace during winter. It felt so overwhelmingly sad, but that became replaced with hot anger and grief, so sharp and painful. It shut Its eyes tight, the world felt like it was spinning.

"See?" The Other Dog said as she paced the fence slowly. "You shouldn't belong to anyone. I think you see that now."

The Dog sat in silence with Its thoughts as The Other Dog walked away. It looked up, and she was gone again as if having never been there, with no scent or trace to leave behind.

She's right. I am no Dog.

The Heart

She lay on the beat-up couch that night, thinking hard. She thought her head would explode. It was dark in the living room, and the Master had retired upstairs getting ready for bed after a brief and silent dinner and an extra long day at work. *If I don't have the Master, will I be alone like how I feel right now?* She takes a look around the empty living room which was dimly lit by the light in the kitchen being the only one left on. She and Her thoughts were the only company She had.

The memories began to stir in Her mind as She closed her eyes. Her mind was replaying the events that led up to this. Despite how painful the memories were and how they made Her feel lost, Her mind was desperate to process and think.

She was taking in one last look at her first home. She sighed, nervous but also very excited about what Her new life would lead to. There appeared a man, someone who She thought She knew well, tall with dark, shiny hair and dark green eyes that had a kind look to them. She looked down with pride at Her recently new collar, which was a luminous pearly white with gems that studded it. It was beautiful. He also gazed upon it, patting her shoulder reassuringly.

"Don't worry, I'll take good care of you."

He winked at Her in a playful manner and She buried Her face in His arm, as She felt an overwhelming love for this man. She tried not thinking about how much leaving Her first home would change Her life, perhaps not for the better.

Later, when they got to The Master's house, which

they now shared, He put on their favorite song and they danced, slow and sweet. He held Her paws in His hands gently, but also with strong hands and a tight grip. She now knew one day that would be used to His advantage. That night He talked in depth about their future with abundant excitement, as She listened, feeling just as thrilled.

This was one of the better memories that made Her heart feel full, but was now bittersweet with the sting of pain that came with it.

The other memory that came to her mind next was shortly after they had gotten into their first fight. She was sitting on the back porch in the Yard, hunched over with tears welling up. She stared at the fence, which at this point was new, and at the time, would avoid going near it. That's what caused the dispute. She had greeted another man at the fence who was friendly, but the Master who had observed them yelled at Her for the first time.

"I was worried he would take you away from me," was his justification.

This memory made Her grit Her teeth. Pulling away from Her intense recollections, She looked down at Her bare neck, the collar She loved had become dirty and all of the gemstones had fallen out of it. The Master couldn't bother to replace it. She reflected on the past few days, and how much had happened. How She had met the Other Dog, and been treated by The Master throughout the years. *I've been trapped,* She realized. *This whole time, when I thought he was freeing me.*

I'm not alone, I have myself.

Her ears perked up when She heard The Master upstairs flick off the light.

He's gone to bed.

The Teeth

Every instinct She had was urging Her along as She

climbed the staircase silently, like She was stalking a squirrel that had found its way into the Yard. She didn't really need to see, She knew Her way around this house even though She had spent the past few years on the couch.

She could see the Master's door illuminated slightly by the moonlight from a window at the top of the staircase to Her left. It was cracked open to Her delight. Her jaws opened to reveal Her deadly sharp fangs as She entered the almost pitch-black room. She could faintly see the shape of The Master lying on one side of the large bed, the other was empty with no pillows. He was breathing deeply in sleep. *Stupid man,* She thought. *He's a dead man in his sleep.*

Licking Her chops, She swiftly lept on the Master with murderous calculation. He screamed in terror as She tore into him without feeling hesitation, sinking Her teeth into his shoulder to disable him as he tried to pry Her off. She was wild.

The sharp taste of his blood sat on her tongue as it spurted from his flesh.

Her teeth tore and his bones crunched as She unleashed Her attack.

His howls of pain made Her even more enraged. *I bet you're scared. You deserve this, after all the pain and sorrow you caused me.* She snarled as She lunged for his throat, fangs cutting through layers of skin with ease. He choked on his own blood as She pulled away, panting with sheer effort.

She looked down at Her hand, spattered and stained crimson by blood, clutching a kitchen knife. She was no Dog, not anymore. She was wild and, better yet, free.

This knowledge haunted Her though, and She wept. Part of Her was horrified and feeling alone, part of Her was relieved. She wiped the tears away and walked away from the corpse that was once Her Master, not looking back.

THE LIVES OF GHOSTS AFTER THEIR LIVES HAVE ENDED

MAGGIE TRABOSH

There is a road. A long road. A long road in a small town, in a big state, in an even bigger country. A long road with houses lining either side of it. The houses are tall and differ in colors, but they all look the same. At the end of the long road, there is a dead-end sign, and next to it is a purple house with lawn gnomes on the porch. There's a car in the driveway, but no lights on in the house. The front door is unlocked. You go in.

The entryway is beautiful. Big windows surround the door, along with a basket of shoes. Lights hang from the ceiling, and a carpet lines the long hallway. The kitchen calls to you. You hear the faint buzzing of the refrigerator and the slight hum of a lamp that has been on for too long. The kitchen is nice. The dishes in the dishwasher are from the dinner party. The coffee is ground in the corner, waiting to be used. You hear a slight alarm.

The connected living room is full of natural light. The blankets are sprawled out on the couch as if someone has just used them, but there's a slight layer of dust sitting on the couch. The walls are covered in art and color, and a paint can sits next to an open spot on the wall. Painter's tape and a brush sit atop, waiting.

The stairs are hardwood, and the alarm gets louder

as you climb. The walls are empty of color but have sticky notes posted on the walls, as if with no sense of direction. The notes seem random:

COLORS?

TOMORROW

CALL. RED??

Going higher up the stairs the sticky notes grow. Now with reminders to get gas, pay the bills, and call people back. You notice none have been done yet though, because the ones that are done get crossed over. Just like the one that says:

~~CLEAN KITCHEN~~

Actually, maybe that means don't do that? Probably when something is done, you can surely just take the sticky note off the wall. Whatever, not your house. The alarm is loud now, weird that it hasn't been turned off yet, right?

You head to the bedroom. You can tell the alarm is coming from here. It feels like the room is shaking. You lose focus. The bedroom follows the same pattern as the living room, colorful, art, and shelves, there is barely a blank space on the wall. On the desk is a bouquet of flowers in a nice small vase to fit the short stems. The alarm is blurring your eyesight, but lucky you, you have 20/20 vision. From what you can see, the bed is a queen with pillows all over the place, but the decorative pillows lay on the floor forgotten from the sleeping person in the bed. Next to the pillows is a green dragon stuffed animal that has quite a lot of wear and tear from all the love its received in its life.

You must turn that alarm off soon. It's screaming at you. Is that your name? Are you hearing your name through the alarm? No, it's just loud and annoying.

Turn it off.

You still hear ringing in your ears. As your ears start to get used to the silence, and your eyes adjust to not being blurry anymore, you see more details about the person sleeping in the bed, she has brown hair and doesn't look any older than 20. As she lays there sleeping you notice something more about her.

She's dead.

Wow. Oh my goodness. What do you do with that information? You just found someone dead! You should report it! Ok, but think for a second, how would you without getting convicted yourself? You broke into this home because the door was unlocked. You shouldn't have gone in in the first place. Why did you go in? Why would you break into someone's home? This is an issue.

You run to the window and look outside, hoping to see someone who could help you. There's no one, no one in the street playing basketball, no one in their cars driving away, no one in their yards, the neighborhood actually seems... deserted? Oh wait, there's someone, oh and another person, and another one, and another one. But who are those people, they aren't the couple across the street, or your childhood best friend. Why are they going into that house?

Go. Run into the street and confront them.

You can't. You don't live here, you're not supposed to know these people, so wait. How do you know these people? Ok, no this is fine, just go-

"Hi!" says a voice from behind you.

Who is that? Who is behind you right now? Why is someone talking to you? Did someone else follow you after you snuck in? You take a deep breath and turn around. Right in your face is a girl, pigtails in her hair and holding a very basic teddy bear in a basket that has blankets to make sure the teddy bear is warm.

You're calm, you're cool, you're collected, now just speak.

You say hello.

"Who are you?" Says the girl, at least you're assuming

it's the girl, cause her mouth didn't move, but she is the only one here.

You get cut off before you can explain.

"Are you new here?" Her mouth is still not moving, but it seems like a voice that would come from a little kid. "I'm Poppy. And I'm 11." And now it's weird, because now it is confirmed that it is the little girl in front of you, who is not actually speaking but is also speaking.

Run for it.

You do. You run down the stairs into the walls, you trip and fall down the stairs, and land head first on the bottom hardwood stair. That should've hurt, but it didn't. No pain, no broken bones? Doesn't seem like anything is damaged, so that's a miracle.

"Hello," says a different voice. A different voice? Another person? Two people have followed you, maybe they're working together.

Open your eyes, and we'll work through this together, let's just open our eyes.

You open your eyes, and lean forward to see a set of legs in front of you, well you're screwed. You close your eyes again, trying to remember how before this all you were doing was being nosey. Sticky notes on the wall, the dishwasher, the lamp, how long has that lamp been on? Whatever, doesn't matter anymore, there's people in this house and you've intruded, and now they're mad.

"Do you need help?" Says the same different voice. They are now called voice B until further notice.

You say no before anyone can say anything else.

"Ok. I was just wondering, goodness." You can tell that voice B has moved, but you don't know where to, cause for some reason you didn't hear any steps? Whatever, that is absolutely not the issue right now.

"Do you think they have any idea what is going on right now?" says the girl, but now she's downstairs? She's with voice B, how did she get down here? You're blocking the stairs, you would've noticed her coming down.

You open your eyes and look over to where they are, and see a very tall man that is wearing clothing like a butler, with a pocket watch in his pocket and everything. The girl is looking up at him, you think they could be best friends.

"I don't think they do, no." He is very quiet, and very aware of the fact that the girl is very opposite of him.

"Ok, well, I'm gonna go meet up with Ruthie." Says the girl.

"Ok. Have fun."

"Thanks, Arthur!"

You get up and say you're leaving, too. Arthur turns his attention to you. He's confused. Why is he confused?

"...Ok? You're a grown adult. You aren't trapped here." Now you're confused. Wasn't he mad at you for breaking and entering? Wasn't he mad that you found that dead body? Is HE mad he found the dead body?! You get up and walk out the door. You expect a cold breeze to hit your shoulders, but nothing happens. Actually, quite the opposite. You are comfortable in the temperature that surrounds you.

You see Poppy run to a house across the street. This is all very weird, and you don't understand what is going on, but as you watch Poppy approach, she walks right through the closed door of the house. And now everything is coming together, why there's no footsteps, why Poppy appeared out of nowhere, why you didn't get hurt rolling down the stairs. These people are ghosts, and you are one too.

You lean your head inside for a moment. You spot Arthur and you get his attention.

"Yes?"

You ask him the dreaded question, the question that you know isn't true. Because ghosts aren't real! They're not real, they're just not.

Ghosts could be real.

"You are a ghost, yes." This was not the answer you were expecting, and now you're at a standstill with the very tall butler man.

You try to thank him, but no words come out. What does one do when they've just learned they're a ghost?

Cry.

You stand in the entryway for a minute longer before Arthur walks up to you.

He puts a hand on your shoulder, and that brings you back. He looks you in the eyes and says, "You should go to Ruthie and Poppy's tea party. They'll be more helpful than you think."

You're sitting at a tea party. Poppy sitting across from you. You're sitting on a child-sized chair, your legs up against your chest, while Poppy fits comfortably. You look around. The tea party is in the attic in the house across the street.

One of the weirdest things about this whole experience is that you don't remember how you died? Or your life before everything. You also have the same tendencies of an alive person, but are dead. For example, you don't have to walk through walls if you don't want to, you can just open the door. Objects don't fall through your hands if you grab them, and you are still a solid being that other people can interact with and touch.

At this tea party is Ruthie, Poppy, an old man named Lester, and a very bright ball of light. A ball of light feels out of place to be in an attic, but you let it slide. You're dead, why are you worrying? Ruthie seems to be the same age, or a little bit younger than Poppy. The attic is covered in coloring pages that have been colored in. Some have been very horribly finished, and some with details and shading. There are boxes in the corner, and cobwebs coating the ceiling.

Arthur told you that Poppy and Ruthie would be helpful, but so far no one has been helpful at all. All anyone has been doing is saying 'wonderful tea' or 'these scones are delicious,' not any backstory to anything!

Talk to Lester, then.

As you turn your attention over to Lester, you watch Poppy turn her stool to speak to the ball of light. Poppy starts having a conversation, asking about the day and the weather. You put this strange exchange to the side and focus on the important things.

You watch Lester take a sip of his imaginary tea, and he turns to look at you. The overhanging shock about the fact that you are dead, and so are all these people, must still be in your facial features because Lester gives you a sympathetic look.

"C'mon kid. Let's go for a walk." Lester stands from the short table, and he looks over to Ruthie, "Ruthie dear, what another wonderful tea party. Lorraine and I will be back next week." Ruthie's smile reaches her eyes with excitement.

"Tell Lorraine to bring her brownies!" She lets out a little squeal of excitement, then turns her attention back to Poppy and the ball of light.

Lester leads you downstairs. You survey your surroundings and see pictures of Lester and his wife, who is most likely Lorraine. The house feels old, with old wallpaper and a very old recliner in the corner with a crocheted blanket on top.

He brings you to the front door and opens it, ushering you out. You take one more look at the house and how different it is from the one you were snooping around this morning. More muted colors, but a lot more love has been in this house. You both walk silently down the street until getting to the four stop intersection. Lester motions to the house across the street. "Steve and Marsha lived there. They were Lorraine and I's best friends in the neighborhood," he sighs out and there's a bit of silence before continuing, "until Marsha passed away, and Steve started to lose himself."

You stay silent. It's always hard to help someone who is in pain. No matter what kind of pain or sadness they might feel. Lester seems to be very sad right now, but maybe he feels content. Maybe he feels ok. Happy, even.

What do you feel right now?

What do you feel right now? You're dead. Fully dead. And yet, you're just standing at the end of the road, listening to Lester, who has been dead longer than you have. So, he must be feeling different things than you are.

"When I died, I woke up here in my bed. I was all alone, but I was here. The community was not as full as it is now, but I'm glad that you get to have a safety net for learning where you are. I did not have the privilege." He stares at the house across the street. And out comes two women with their arms linked together, laughing. Lester grows a small smile.

"That's Marsha and my wife, Lorraine." You look at the women. They have gray hair and crow's feet around their eyes from smiling. They look content, they look ok, they look happy. "After Marsha died, I died a few weeks later. Two completely different circumstances, just unfortunate timing on our parts."

You want to ask more questions, but you can tell that he's going to tell you everything you need to know.

"When you die. you are put in the house that means the most to you, which is why others have an attachment to the house. The house I'm in was mine and Lorraine's most recent home. Lorraine showed up a few years later, and she was as excited as ever." Lorraine and Marsha head straight towards you and Lester, probably to say hello and keep going. "Steve never showed up here." Lester's speaking again caught you off guard. He starts speaking again before you can ask the very obvious question you want to ask.

"We don't know if he's still alive. We don't know if he's somewhere else. He's not here. But we are." Lester looks at you. His face is blank. He doesn't look like he feels anything right now. "I know you probably have a lot of questions. I promise I'm here to listen and answer them. I might be a grumpy old man, but I'm a grumpy old man that's dead. And has been dead much longer than you have. Just stop by." He grabs Lorraine's hand and walks with her back to their home. You watch Marsha walk home alone.

The big ball of light exits Lester's home and floats over to the house three down from Marsha's home.

Go talk to it!

You rush over to the ball of light that now, when you have a closer look, is mesmerizing. The primary colors are white and yellow, with secondary colors of purple and orange. The beams of light that come off are different lengths and move as if breathing. It looks as if it's vibrating too.

You speak to the orb of light, and as the sunsets, the light never dims from this entity in front of you. It takes you a minute to figure out what to say, or to ask, but you gain some confidence.

You ask what they are, hoping not to offend. And you become pleasantly surprised by the conversation you have. The orb does not speak, but makes a humming noise at different pitches that sounds like a song. You understand the orb though. You understand the words it tries to speak with the hums and sounds it makes.

"My name is Tilly. And I am dead just like you," says Tilly. "When you die. You may choose how you would like to be perceived. Through body or soul. I chose soul." If Tilly could, she would be smiling. You can tell by how her pitches differ with emotion. Happiness gets louder and higher, while sadness and anger get lower and quieter.

You tell her you don't remember getting to choose if you wanted to be soul or body. Would you have chosen soul?

It stays silent for a moment. Maybe you've asked a stupid question. Before you can tell her that you take it back she responds. "You had a choice. I promise." She then starts to move the opposite direction of you to her own home.

You walk back to the house where you started, and you stand on the porch and watch all the people interact with one another. The amount of love they all have and the experiences that they all feel together.

All these people are old. All these people have either died from old age or some kind of disease that got them later in life. But these people lived their lives to the very fullest because they got to live it for such a long time.

Except for Poppy. Except for Ruthie. They're just children, and yet they seem pretty content. How did they become so content with being dead even though they're so young?

You take a moment and think of yourself. How old are you? Did you live your life to the very fullest? Did you live it for a long time? Were you loved? Did you have a wife? A husband? Children? Do they miss you?

For the first time since this whole situation, you feel sad. You don't know anything about who you truly were. You only know who you are now, and you want to know what your life was like. You walk into the house, and suddenly, everything has changed. Now, it all starts to feel...familiar.

You stand in the entryway and examine what is happening around you. There are pictures on the walls of family members and children. One of the children has a cowlick in their hair, a beaming smile, and beautiful eyes.

It's you. This is your childhood home.

You sit down on a wooden bench that is absolutely not strong enough to hold a person, but a ghost person, sure. And then you cry. Through this whole fiasco, emotion has been nonexistent, more just numb, so to feel anything at all is overwhelming.

Arthur shows up in the entryway. He notices your situation and sits next to you.

"I know this is very weird. And I know you don't know anything. And I know that you're probably scared. And I bet it's weird that I, of all people, am comforting you. But you can know that we'll take care of you. All of us have been exactly where you are right now. And I bet you that even the people that have been here for a while still feel what you're feeling." You stay silent.

You ask Arthur what this place is to him. Why is he here? What does it mean to him? Was this his childhood home, too?

"This was the first house that I bought with my husband. We moved quite a few times, but this spot was my favorite." You nod in understanding. It's silent again. "I've been here for 14 years. I've been waiting for him. But I realized maybe this house didn't mean the same thing to him as it did to me."

You stay silent. It's just like Steve and Marsha. You ask him if he's alone here. You're concerned he might say yes, and then you'll have to face the truth if you're alone here.

"If you mean alone in the fact that none of my family is here, then yes. But I'm not alone here." He interrupts your upcoming next thoughts. "I have Poppy. And Kathrine, and Michael, and Lester, and Penelope, and Stan. A lot of them don't have family here either. So we stick together. Don't get me wrong, I would love for my husband to be here, or our daughter, but I'm getting by just fine without them."

You thank him for telling you. Opening up to a stranger

can be very odd, and yet everyone in this town seems to be doing all right with doing so. You tell him about how you're having a hard time with who you are and who you have. You don't expect an answer from him, but he breaks the silence.

"Well. Go figure it out."

You didn't think it was that easy, so you tell him that. And he gives you a small chuckle.

"Oh, it's not. But you gotta start somewhere," he stands from the bench and looks towards the hallway. "And I think you should start by exploring the house that you do know." Arthur struts away and lets you sit in silence for a moment.

You walked through the house with a new sense of being dead. With the idea that everything is fine, while everything is absolutely not fine. The walls are lined with art projects you did as a kid and pictures of your family and friends. Drawings made with crayons and markers replace the sticky notes on the walls.

You go to the room where the alarm was previously coming from. It's been transformed into your childhood room, toys in baskets, clothes on the floor, and a chore chart on the wall with star stickers. You can remember your mom putting them up when you brushed your teeth all on your own.

You sit on the bed and stare out the window at the other houses. You close your eyes. You imagine your life from that point of childhood, going to high school, going to college? Or going straight to work. Did you drop out? Or did you graduate? You keep imagining and make it to your death.

Do you really want to see your death right now? To see where you were? What you had? Or even what you lost? You take a breath in and out.

Focus.

Painting Bones

Alizah Carrillo

Content Warnings:
Murder, graphic depictions of violence

The air was cool and the sun's rays were warm, almost welcoming. The sidewalks along the neighborhood were showered by vibrant pink petals, it was perfect. Not as perfect as ImJuu's boyfriend, EunTae, was to her. Today was their one-month anniversary. ImJuu had always fantasized about having a boyfriend, but not just any boy. Growing up, she would watch romance movies in the living room; staring endlessly at the silver screen. Eventually, she got into Korean dramas with her grandma and would watch a new series with her every time she got to visit. Though she was born in America, she never felt like she belonged there. At the time, K-pop hadn't hit America so she had little to no friends to talk about her ikemen (pretty boys) with. Now, she lives in Tongyeong with her grandmother, watching Korean dramas every night. Though her parents were hesitant, she bribed them with good grades, homemade meals, and the longest slide show to ever exist. They swore they aged a few years during that presentation.

EunTae only lived a few blocks from the school, so she would often meet with him and walk to school together. ImJuu turned the corner and arrived at EunTae's apartment complex. He was usually up by now waiting for her. Her gaze darted across the area to find him surrounded by stray dogs.

From the pack of strays, EunTae's head popped up. He wore a charming smile with a glittering stare as he waved at her. He looked so perfect, just like the main lead from the romance Korean drama she had been watching with her grandma, Cha Eun-woo. The mysterious luscious raven locks, plump lips, dark eyes, jawline, and tight waistline. Thinking about it sent her heart into a frenzy, getting her all giddy inside.

"EunTae? What are you doing with all these strays? Awww," she cooed.

"I tend to feed the strays around here whenever I make soup. I always have leftover bones and some meat scraps. Might as well give it to the strays around here, better than letting it rot in the trash," he explained, looking down at the dogs gnawing at the bones.

He's hot, he's kind, and he's an animal lover! Her stomach was tied in a knot.

"We should get going or we'll be late." He grabbed her wrist, leading her as they walked around the feasting strays. Walking slightly behind him, she stared down at her wrist which EunTae still held. His hands are bigger. Her lips curled into a smile. Something about that new knowledge made her happy. She felt as if she was being looked at. Lifting her head, she met EunTae's gaze. Was he watching the entire time? Embarrassing. He didn't say anything. His grip loosened and slid into her palm. His fingers intertwined with hers. She was caught off guard. Her face felt hot, her head was fuzzy, her stomach light. In her peripheral vision, she spotted the school entrance a few meters away.

"Wah, l-look we're here" She stumbled over her words as she pulled herself away from his grip. Her pace fastened until she yielded in front of the school's entrance.

"Didn't know you were excited for school today, thought you hated it," EunTae spoke with an amused tone. ImJuu yanked her head back towards him.

"I have track practice after school so don't wait for me. I'll text you." He placed his palm on top of her head. His expression was sweet and was accompanied by his famous soft charming smile. Her face glowed red as she looked down at her feet. She let out a hum of agreement before EunTae walked away.

The next day, EunTae didn't come to their usual meeting spot, causing ImJuu to worry. She wandered around the school halls hoping to find him. However, after 20 minutes of searching, it was unsuccessful.

In an empty classroom, she sat at a desk alone.

"Did I do something? Did he go home without me?" she mumbled to herself.

Faint singing rang from the hallways stopping ImJuu from her thoughts. Following the sound, she found herself in front of the art room. Pushing the sliding door aside, she peeked into the room.

"EunTae? What are you doing here, I thought we were supposed to walk home together," she spoke shyly. His face seemed to flush red as he pulled the canvas in front of him closer towards himself.

"Ah! I'm sorry, I must've lost track of time," he admitted, stumbling over his words. His eyes were soft, eyebrows furrowed. His face was flushed. Was he embarrassed? ImJuu had never seen him like this before, she felt as if she was in a shojo anime.

A giggle escaped her lips, a wide smile appeared on her face.

"What are you painting?" she asked, a sly expression creeping upon her face as she crept up from behind him.

The canvas was unfinished and was a bit abstract. It was a woman; it was her.

She had no words but managed to shoot him a

flattered smile. "It's beautiful."

"Thanks. We should head home, it's getting late," he suggested, getting up from his seat as he collected the paint-covered brushes.

"Here, let me help." She began grabbing the cups filled with paint and water mixtures. She jumped when she felt her side bump into the table that held the paint. The palette flung and paint splattered. She let out a gasp and looked over at the canvas, worried for the worst. The painting was altered, it had random splotches of green and red paint. Worried, she stood in front of the canvas speechless. EunTae looked over at her, his eyes widening. He pushed her away from the painting causing her to stumble over and fall onto the floor. A stinging pain came from her wrist when she tried to push herself back up in disbelief.

"E-EunTae I'm sorry, I didn't mean to..."

He stood speechless as he stared down at his new painting. His hands curled into fists, his knuckles white. "What the fuck ImJuu." His voice was stern, his brows creased, eyes filled with irritation as he turned to her. His glare sent shivers down her body. For the first time, she was afraid to be alone with EunTae.

He ran his fingers through his hair, before placing his palms on his hips. "Just go home ImJuu," he sighed, unable to look at her.

"EunTae... I'm sorry, please calm down." She shuddered. Despite the pain in her wrist, she hid it and pushed herself up from the floor. She gripped her injured wrist with her other hand to suppress the pain.

"I said go home! You're fucking pathetic," he shouted this time.

Tears began to form in her eyes, before she could compose herself, one fell after another down her cheek. She turned and grabbed her school bag. Running out of the room, she slammed the sliding door on her way out.

ImJuu spent the rest of the day shut in her room, crying into her pillow.

"ImJuu are you okay in there?" Her grandmother knocked on the door. No response. "Why don't you come eat dinner with grandma, it's lonely eating alone don't you think?" she suggested.

The door opened revealing ImJuu in her pajamas and with hair that looked like a rat's nest. Her face was puffy and her nose was red, most likely from blowing it constantly. ImJuu nodded and walked into the kitchen with her grandmother.

"I won't ask what happened but I take it it's that young man you're always with. Whatever it is, food heals the soul. I even made your favorite." She smiled, placing a bowl of mandu soup in front of her. ImJuu began to cry again, sniffling as she devoured the soup and the banchan along with it. ImJuu's phone rang from her bedroom.

"EunTae...? No, I'm sorry! Yes, I can be there in five minutes!" her tone began to lift. "Grandmother-" she managed to get out before her grandmother interrupted.

"Don't worry about me, I was young too," she chuckled. ImJuu smiled and hugged her grandmother before running into her room to change. Four minutes later, she found herself in front of an abandoned building.

She wondered if he had sent her the wrong address. Suddenly she felt a hand placed on top of her shoulder. Afraid, she let out a shriek and slapped the owner of the hand. "EunTae! I'm so sorry!" she apologized when she turned to see him.

"Heh... I deserved that." He let out a half chuckle wincing a bit from the sting her palm left on his face.

"What did you want to show me?" she wondered, looking back at the haunting building.

"Close your eyes. Trust me." He smiled, placing a blindfold around her head and taking her hand. He led her up a few short steps and into the building. "I'm a bit embarrassed, you're the first I've taken here before," he said, removing her blindfold.

It took a couple of binks for her vision to recover. Her eyes widened and a smile appeared across her face. Multiple painted portraits and landscapes were placed around the building, some hanging on the brittle wall and some leaning against the walls on the floor. In the middle of all of these paintings, there was a painting stool holding a particularly familiar painting. It was the portrait of her that she had seen earlier that day except it was finished. It was less abstract this time and more realistic. The painting exhibited elegant soft lighting, bringing out her soft features. It was warm-colored and breathtaking.

"EunTae..." she murmured, looking back at him as he squeezed her hand gently. He placed his index finger on top of his lips and pointed up at the ceiling. It was the stars, showing through a large hole in the crumbling ceiling.

She felt so moved and entranced, she felt like she was in a romance novel. He really was... perfect.

"I want to make another painting for you, I left some paint downstairs, could you grab it for me?" he asked, pulling an apron above his head. She nodded obediently and skipped towards the stairs. It was dark, she felt around for the switch and found it in an odd spot. She flicked it on and it took a few seconds for the light to work. The light bulb illuminated the room revealing multiple paintings similar to the one he painted of her except each was a different woman.

Her heart shattered. Who are these women? She turned around to leave but froze when she saw EunTae holding a bat. When did he follow her down? She hadn't heard a single step.

"Don't take it personally," he cooed, wearing an unnatural smile. She took a step back in fear before running towards the space to the right of him. She was stopped when she felt his hand grab ahold of a chunk of her hair. "What the fuck do you think you're doing?" He spoke in a stern tone, his gaze striking fear into her. That was the last memory she had before he threw her down the stairs.

Now she sat in a chair, in a small room, a shed perhaps. Where is this? Am I dead? Memories of what happened began to flood her mind again. Her gaze scanned the dark room she was in. In her peripheral vision, she found a woman's body next to her, except it was in parts. She recognized her face from one of the paintings she saw. A deafening shriek escaped her lungs, as she pushed herself up from the chair only to meet the floor within seconds. Her legs were shattered. The pain started to set in as she looked at her wounds. She swiped her hands across her abdomen and limbs, trying to clean the blood off her hands. Weak in her stomach, she lost the little food she had that day. I'm alive, why?

Thoughts of survival filled her head as she scanned the room for an exit. A staircase that led to the door in the corner was visible; however, she couldn't stand. Her legs, she couldn't feel or move them. She heard creaking floorboards from the other side of the door. Someone was on the other side.

"Help, please! My name is ImJuu, I've been kidnapped! Please call the police!" she called out desperately, as tears of hope formed in her eyes. The door began to open slowly.

"Hold on I'm coming," an old man's voice came through the door.

"Thank you god..." she whispered to herself. Relief was fleeting as a wave of adrenaline hit her.

The door rattled before creaking open, it revealed EunTae. "Surprise! Happy to see me?" He laughed, holding his arms out as if he was a pleasant sight. In one hand he held a machete. His face was deranged, nothing like a human—eyes squinted, corners of his lips curled upward unnaturally. ImJuu's heart skipped a beat and her body began to tremble. "Why? Were you expecting someone else? That hurts y'know. You're supposed to be loyal to me," he growled, his expression and voice becoming serious. He approached ImJuu, grabbed her arm, and pulled her close. "Was it not what you were expecting? All you international girls are the same. As long as a guy portrays a character similar to your romance novels, you'll date anyone." He laughed. ImJuu continued to sob uncontrollably as EunTae irritated and turned angry. "You don't seem to listen. There is no point talking to a corpse anyways," he sighed, pulling the blade up to her throat.

"Fuck you, men like you are the worst!" she yelled, struggling to put distance between them.

"Hah. Maybe I am, but it does feel good" he chuckled. "I did love you, I really did but in the end, you're just like them." He pulled her into a kiss, her first and last one. The blade he held to her neck now penetrated her abdomen. It hurt, but her heart hurt more. Her vision grew blurry, and then there was nothing.

The next day was sunny just like any other day. EunTae sat outside the apartment complex he lived in, being greeted by the usual pack of strays. He pulled out a plastic bag full of bones. As he fed them, a young girl approached him. Her uniform was from a different school, but she looked like a first-year student.

"Oppa, could I get your number?"

Ghost of Our Machine

Quintana Franklin

Bless me, Father. It's been two weeks since my last confession. I seek your advice. I have had strange dreams lately and they're beginning to worry me.

I had the first one a few weeks ago. I saw people wearing strange clothes. They looked extremely tight and uncomfortable. All the men wore hats and all the women wore these poofy dresses. They all looked so...rigid. They were walking in nature, but it didn't look natural. All the plants were cut unusually neat and the grass was short and thin, not like the thick White-root I'm used to. It looked just like the people. As I watched them, the landscape would jump up and down, a blip in their stroll, but no one seemed to notice. After some of the jumps, it was as if the people would repeat what they had just done over again. And I didn't see any color, even in all the nature! No color at all. No noise either. The people moved their lips, but I didn't hear anything at all.

The next one had people too, but the world was brighter. The sky poured out all sorts of chroma. They spun, and there was a sun in the sky, but it was shiny, and the light bounced off it. The people were covered in chroma, too. And they didn't look rigid at all. I don't think any of them ever stopped moving. The people spun too, intense and dazzling. They were all close together, and they moved their bodies all over. And the clothes. They wore almost nothing. Some of it was tight, others loose, and some of it was even shiny and sparkled in the lights. Oh, and the noise was atrocious! Not like the last dream. There were so many people talking and laughing, and music came from all over, like the air was made of it. But it wasn't any music I'd ever heard before. It was loud and heavy. I couldn't tell you what instrument the noises came from.

The next dream I had was a few days later. I didn't see people in this one. There were long lines of something; they almost looked like buildings, but they were small and shiny, and they moved on wheels, but not any wheels I've ever seen. They weren't wooden like our wagons, but something else. They rolled along in these big lines all on their own. Nothing was pulling or pushing them, they just moved. Oh, and the lines went on as far as I could see. And there were colors again! These were brighter and they hurt my eyes a little when I looked at them. I could see metal giants in the distance too. They were tall and slender and their necks stuck out, almost as long as their body. I've never seen so much metal in my life. They moved objects that no human could lift, big ones like they were building a big house. It was incredible.

I've never dreamt of things like this before. It's all so very foreign and unnatural. In most of them, there's remarkably little green, like the world isn't even there anymore. Here, there's green everywhere, and there's gold in the spelt fields and everything grows wild. The only place there isn't green is in our homes and on the paths worn by wagons. The shape of the Earth itself didn't even look the same. The only flat places on Gaia are the grasslands, there are hills everywhere else and rough, gritty rocks the color of evening rain clouds that sprout from the soil. The rocks I see are dull, not like the leussanite and nieive cleaiba we have. There were no Sand Sycamores along the rivers or Felonwood Oak in the forests or the Spotted Queen Baobabs on the grasslands. The trees in my dreams were oddly shaped, some were even pointy and sharp. Should I be worried that all these odd things come from my mind? Is this a sign of something more serious, or just my imagination?

Bless me Father, it's been a week since my last confession.

I had another dream last night. It was horrid. I saw flashes of light, the ground shook beneath me, and there were screams and everything was so loud it was like my skull was shaking with each concussive blast. People were running, more people than I've ever seen. Some were running and some of them were thrown with the light. Those screams have stayed with me since. Just echoes, but they make my heart hurt. I've never seen such awful things. I've seen death, I've seen sickness, I've seen a man gone mad, I've even helped slaughter the livestock, but this was different. This was worse than death. Why? Why would I dream of something like this? Why would I dream of so much death and despair unless there is something truly wrong with me?

Bless me, Father. It's been two weeks since my last confession.

I know you told me that we all have nightmares and that I shouldn't worry, but I've had more. Several, actually. Over the past two weeks, I've had these dreams every night. Some of them are calm like they used to be, but others wake me in tears. I've woken up my parents a few times and my mother has started to worry. I find that I'm no longer the same when I'm awake either. The things I see live behind my eyes and I remember the terrors and my body shakes because they haunt me so. I wish they'd stop. I fear

I've upset the Mother somehow to be seeing these things. If not that, then I must be truly twisted.

Bless me, Father. It's been three weeks since my last confession.

I have tried all the remedies you gave me, and all of your suggestions, but none of them worked. I'm still getting these dreams. I'm so confused. Even the ones that are peaceful are perplexing. They have contraptions and buildings I never thought could exist. In my waking hours, I've never imagined anything close to this, but when I'm asleep I see inconceivable things. Some of them are truly wonderful—buildings that touch the heavens, hundreds of people joining in song and dance, and colors exploding in the atmosphere, rattling the gates of heaven. Even the awful ones are impossible. There was one where I was in the sky in a sort of moving box. I was so far up I could barely make out the ground. I saw fire and smoke climb upward like mountains forming before my eyes. It billowed towards me and almost touched the flying box. It was coming up in a column and then spreading, its shape like a mushroom. Such a thing isn't possible! Neither are flying boxes. I feel... lost, I guess. I just don't know what to do. What should I do?

Bless me, Father. It's been two days since my last confession.

I had a new dream. It was different from the others. I saw a wall covered in stars—an array of tiny lights. The stars blinked and a small rectangle on the wall showed changing words. Another rectangle showed lines and dots, and they were moving too. The whole dream I watched the wall change. Walls don't change, not like that. But it wasn't the wall that surprised me. I heard a voice, right next to my ear. It was a woman. She said hello, and that she was here to help me. Her voice was normal...almost. It was so crisp and clear. She enunciated all her words and didn't make any mistakes. It was steady and there wasn't any emotion. I can't put my finger on what it was, but it was unsettling. Like when you look at your reflection in water and ripples shift it so it waves and distorts it a little, Taking your image and twisting it just slightly so it's just barely not you anymore. Not wrong, but not right. I'm getting tired of these dreams. I just want to sleep in peace.

Bless me, Father. It's been almost two weeks since my last confession.

The woman is in my dreams more often now. She asks me questions that I don't want to answer. She asked which colony I landed on. I didn't know what she meant. I don't know of any colonies on Gaia, only the Provinces. She asked me if I'd found her vid-ay-os educational. I don't know what a vid-a-o is. She speaks nonsense most of the time. Using words I've never heard and talking about things that don't make sense. She talks of all these countries, but in a way that doesn't make sense. She's said that countries did things. But the country can't do something, it's a place not a person, it can't make decisions or choices. I don't understand.

*

The woman continues to taunt me. But she's not real, she's just a dream so why do I hear her? Has the sacred soil of our Mother forsaken me? Does my own planet reject me? I think Father Barton is suspicious. He might bring me before the Mother in a trial. If I hear someone telling me that Mother Nature is not the only path I would be labeled a heretic. No. No, I write it here, and I'll hide it where they won't find it. But I have to write it down. I need something to keep myself sane. Something. Why does she speak to me? I've never forsaken our Mother! Never.

I'm still having these dreams. Sometimes she speaks, and sometimes I just see. She's spoken of machines and teknologee. Things that move on their own, but those aren't real. But I see them. In my dreams. I've never been creative or imaginative, my parents always said I was built for farming like that. I've never thought up things like this. They aren't real. How could they be? But the other option is they're in my head. She's in my head and I made her. Then I truly would be a heretic.

I try not to sleep because I know the dreams will come, but I sleep anyway. No matter how hard I try my body gives in. Or maybe it's my mind. Maybe I want to dream deep down, maybe I want to see these things, maybe

"..receive.."

"...Hello? Mom?...Dad?"

"..adjust...do you receive?"

"Is somebody there? Hello?" My voice is shaking. That voice, it's her.

"Hello,"

I think I've lost my mind entirely. She just spoke to me.

I heard her in the garden, by the well. I was awake, and I heard her. She was quiet and I could only hear some of what she was saying, but I heard her. I was awake. I was writing when it happened. This is the only proof I have that I wasn't dreaming. I have to have this journal with me all the time now. If I hear her, I can write so I can know if I was dreaming. I just want her to leave me alone.

"Do you receive?"

"You again." I pull out my journal to record that she's

speaking to me. The words are jagged and smudged as they appear on the page as my hand shakes.

"My calculations were correct. I can now communicate with you while you are in this state." My forehead tightens, and my jaw clenches. I take an unsure breath.

"Who are you?" My chest tightens as I say it. What if she says nothing? What if she says my name? What if

"I am Ava." Ava. Ava?

"Why are you talking to me? Why are you telling me these things?" I can feel my pulse in my stomach, the pinpricks of sweat building on my skin as I grip the pages of my journal.

"So you do not forget." My grip falters amidst my confusion.

"Forget? Forget what?" My voice feels louder when I hear it, but not stronger.

"History."

"Hist-" I catch myself for a moment as I hear wheels hitting rocks on the road. I watch a steer appear behind a tree, and the wagon it pulls slowly follows. I wait until they round the bend in the road before I speak again.

"History? What are you talking about? What do the dreams mean? What am I seeing?" I look around me, hoping to see her.

"You are seeing my records. I possess an exabyte of videos and various other file types of historical records from Terra Prime."

"Terra Prime?"

"Terra Prime, originally known as Earth."

"Ee-arth? Like, soil?"

"Earth. A planet in the Sol System. Origin planet of the human species." My breath stops in my throat before it can exit my mouth. My lips feel as though they're stuck together, my saliva like glue on my tongue.

"No. No, we're on Gaia. Humans are from Gaia. We're

on Gaia."

"Gaia was named one of the destination colonies in the exodus from Earth. Located in the Proxima Centauri system, Gaia is approximately 4.2 light years away." My breath catches in my throat. I pry my lips open to speak again.

"You're lying. How would you know any of this? You're lying!" My voice builds as anger replaces confusion. She can't know any of this. We're from Gaia. No one has ever spoken about humans on other planets. I've never heard of Earth. She's lying, she has to be. The Father wouldn't lie to me, my parents wouldn't lie to me. My people wouldn't lie. If there are other humans out there, why wouldn't we want to know them?

"I am programmed to assist you, I am not capable of disinformation. I was installed on the ship destined for this colony to assist the crew and passengers on their voyage."

"If any of that were true, don't you think I would've heard of any of it? Don't you think we'd know where we came from? How we got here?" I'm almost screaming now. Screaming at the empty air as her voice speaks to me again. She's trying to deceive me. But, that means I have to be crazy, right? Crazy enough to make all of this up? All the impossible things.

"The crew and passengers aboard the S.S. Donner voted to purge all history of Earth and technological knowledge upon arriving at the colony. They decided it would be best to begin humanity again." Liar.

"Then why are you telling me? If they voted to forget, why make me remember?"

"The archivist aboard the ship programmed me to circumvent the vote after an appropriate amount of time had passed and ensure historical records were recovered. Your brain waves were the most receptive to my signals."

"I don't believe you. If there were a ship here, we'd know about it." The words barely leave my lips. It's as if the confident voice in my head is muffled, my faith faltering. If she's lying, I'm crazy. I don't want to be crazy.

"If you would like proof of the S.S. Donner's existence, please follow my directions to its landing site."

I finally come upon a cave. Its walls are hard and almost shine in the waning sunlight.

"Turn right and walk 100 meters." She says. The Father would not approve of this. The Father didn't really approve of the dreams either. But why would I trust her? She's given me no reason to, and what she says can't possibly be true. But, if she is telling the truth, then my mind is sound. If all this is real, then it is not my thoughts that are tainted with this lunacy. This is the only way to prove it. I take one last breath of the fresh air and walk through the threshold.

The air is stagnant and musty. The floor is hard like rock, but it's smooth underneath my feet. It feels almost like ice, but not quite that slippery. I take smaller steps, bracing my hand against the wall unsure of what the ground will do if I misstep. My footsteps echo along a hallway in front of me. The light from my lantern bounces off the walls and out of the corner of my eye, I see something darker streaked along the wall. I hold the light up and there it is, in bold, black letters. S.S. Donner.

The ship is real. I steady myself with a few more breaths before I continue down the path in front of me. The shadows move along the edges of my lantern warping the path into a boulevard of twisted branches and hands grasping, pushing me along to whatever fate the ship holds for me. I cross another threshold at the end. The room is dark. A wall covered in bumps, like notches in treebark. I press one and it recedes into the wall and emits a quiet click before bouncing back out again. I take a couple of steps back. This is the wall from my dream when she first spoke to me. But there are no stars this time.

"Welcome to the S.S. Donner." A voice chimes from all around me, almost as if coming from the walls themselves. I nearly jump out of my skin.

"Ava?" I whisper into the dark.

"Hello." Her voice responds, louder than I've ever heard it, but fuzzy around the edges. A small unnatural light appears on a table in front of me--a star.

"How much of what you said was true? About Earth?"

"Everything I have told you is the truth." A breath.

"What about what you showed me?" Suddenly the room erupts, a torrent of light hitting my eyes. I bring my arms up to shield my face.

"These are my historical records on humanity." I try to open my eyes but can only squint. It's like looking into the sun itself. I look to my left and on a small rectangle, I see the people with no color walking through the grass. I look to my left and there is the cloud of fire and smoke in the sky. There are so many rectangles, all of them showing my dreams, and some of them show new things. I don't remember moving them, but my arms are at my sides now. I look from dream to dream, rectangle to rectangle. So many and so bright.

"What is this?" I ask Ava. My voice barely squeezes through my tight throat, my chest constricting around my heart.

"These are your ancestors. This is where you come from."

"All these things, all those horrible things you showed me...what they did to each other? How could anybody do all this?"

"Humanity's innovation is the reason for the need for exodus from Earth. It is also the reason you were able to travel to Gaia."

"What happened to Earth?" Images flash in front of me. More fire and smoke, strange moving things, people, the ground, water, maps.

"Your ancestral home is barren. Harvested, neglected, and scarred beyond repair. The air, water, and ground were all contaminated until they became toxins. There was nothing left for humanity to consume, and no more territory to spread to, so they needed to leave."

"How could they do that? Mother is the only way of life, without her we couldn't survive!" Pressure builds in my eyes as I watch a planet burn, watch creatures who look like me poison and kill a world.

"Their innovation and ambition is the reason your species fled its home. Their innovation is also the reason you're here. The reason the colonies exist. The reason any survived the death of Earth." The dreams continue in front of me, horrors and marvels beyond reckoning.

"Please stop." The dreams keep going. I don't think she heard me.

"Please stop!" I say it a little louder. The dreams are starting to burn my eyes, like steam hitting them.

"Based on my data, it is the human condition to build creations beyond imagination, then destroy them. To tear down humanity's glory because you did not build it. To pave over the ruins of the cure and build a monument to peace and unity. To banish all heretics for remembering the glory that once stood in its place."

"Please stop!" I'm yelling now, and I feel tears on my cheeks. I will my arms to cover my eyes, to stop the burning, but they don't move. The images continue to flash in front of me, the light from the rectangles becoming a torrid blight, my eyes beginning to itch, the pain urging my hands to claw at my eyes. The people with no color in the grass again. Even they seem twisted and malevolent now. These are not dreams. Nightmares, all of them nightmares. I wish I'd never listened to her, never followed her to this place.

"Do you wish to forget? If you choose to forget you erase all of history. *Your* history. All of humanity's faults, glories, and all its history have culminated in *you*. You are human. This is *you*."

A breath and burning eyes, mind crying for muscles to move. I look at what my ancestors have done. What *we've* done.

"Do you choose to forget?"

What I Left in the Woods

Robyn Holley

Content Warnings:
Animal neglect, depression, implied racism

There is no place or time more haunted than New England in the fall. Take it from an opinionated New Englander who has seen very little of the outside world. This naive but stubborn opinion is as unshakable as the mottled granite foundation of my childhood home. My confidence in the unmatchable spookiness of my rural home comes from a meager twenty-nine years of hopelessly cold toes, gloomy gray skies, the endless density of dark evergreen forests, old graveyards filled with skinny, crumbling brown headstones, and the seasonal depression that inevitably starts to creep in at the first turn of a golden leaf and ends sometime after the last patch of ice melts. *If* the ice ever melts, that is.

Yup, it's all cold weather and cold people in New England. The people are standoffish and like to be left to their own devices. If you're a stranger, that is. Once you've proven your worth, or your literal usefulness, or perhaps a few ancestral documents–or at the very least, proof of residence–the outer crust of a salty New Englander starts to crack and the heart of gold shines through like sunbeams through the gray and purple clouds overhead.

I'm from a little rural town in New Hampshire called Lyndeborough. Pronounced *line-burrow*. Not *lind-burrow* or *lindie-burrow*. Large area, small population. People in the next town have never heard of the place. Nevertheless, Lyndeborough persists through years of rough weather and the rigidity of tradition. There is one brick-and-mortar business in Lyndeborough–the general store in the town center. Shabby-looking on the outside, the boxy white building is crammed full of local merchandise and convenience store wares. The town locals convene there to buy cigarettes and exchange gossip about the intimate and mysterious happenings of a small community. Lyndeborough only has one of everything at most, and everything is distinct in appearance, identity, and function. One red brick library. One white steepled church. One defunct railroad track. One wooden bench, one antique cannon. Citizens' Hall. Not the town hall, no one uses that anymore. Citizens' Hall is an all-purpose building that serves as a meeting place for the board of selectmen, houses the town police department, and boasts a large event space upstairs with creaky wooden floors, a tiny stage, and high ceilings. After high school, I briefly rented the space to give lessons in Cape Breton step dancing. I still have the key somewhere.

Since Lyndeborough lacks the economic opportunity and excitement of the "big city" (meaning Nashua, pronounced *nash*-you-wuh), oddities and local legends are treasured novelties often brought out in the cold months to combat the seasonal depression. I like to refer to Lyndeborough as a semi-fictional place because of its larger-than-life characters, its elusive wildlife, and its oddball locals. For instance, there's Farmer John. Lots of rural communities have a Farmer John. Ours has long legs, slightly stooped shoulders, a full head of white hair, deep creases in his face, and bushy eyebrows over bright blue eyes–but curiously, no beard hiding his hound-dog cheeks, sun spots, and the lump of clay that is his nose. Farmer John likes the ladies, and he makes it no secret. By now he's probably pissed off half the town's population with his crass humor and irreverent attempts at flirtation, but the same people he pisses off will still proudly assert their acquaintance with him and share their stories of the things he said, the fish he caught, the skunk he shot, the corn he planted, or the calf he named Peanut. I have my own stories, of course, having lived next door to the obnoxious animal–and Peanut, too.

Everyone who lived on my road was an oddity for some reason or another. It was a way of life in Lyndeborough. There was the lady who dressed up her plastic lawn flamingos in seasonal attire, the man who sent out yearly postcards about March of the Dimes, and the two shaggy-headed teen boys who swung at each other with some sort of medieval weapon. My other next-door neighbors were a British music teacher who was the embodiment of a stiff upper lip, his hippie American wife who practiced alternative medicine, and their three teenagers who embraced their mother's Bahá'í Faith and wore metal pendants to combat radiation from their cell phones.

My family was just as strange as anyone else who lived on my road. It was just Mom and me, and my mother said that two people didn't really constitute a family. We didn't even match. I had my late father's dark, tight curls and what my cousin William called "the year-round tan." In a place like Lyndborough, that "tan" really stands out. My mother had a few light brown freckles scattered over her pale skin. She had long, wavy red hair and blue eyes which I envied as a child. If our contrasting physical features and lack of a family patriarch weren't odd enough, my mother also made her own colloidal silver and subscribed to magazines distributed by non-denominational cults. That's probably why we ended up moving to Lyndeborough in the first place. It's the place to live if you're a bit odd.

My mother's thought process swung wildly between logic and absurdity. Over her thirty-year nursing career, she developed a glowing reputation for consistency, procedure, and keeping a cool head during emergencies. Outside of work, she was a paranoid nonconformist and an unyielding pessimist. She never married, but raised me as a quasi-Christian snob, insisting on homeschooling me throughout high school while avoiding other homeschoolers. She took the Bible as literally as she could and fixated on the verses about disobedient children and generational curses. She distrusted and disliked organized religions, doctors, pharmacies, scientists, the United Nations, and waiters. Those poor waiters. My mother had the personality of the black bears we saw trundling through the woods on occasion. She kept to herself, slept a lot during the cold months, and growled whenever anyone got too close. She was also a fiercely protective parent. An honest-to-goodness mama bear. Anyone who knew my mother knew better than to mess with me. If Farmer John had known the danger that lurked next door, he never would have risked those comments about my "hooters."

Mom and I lived in the upper half of a little blue house with my Maine Coon cat Peter, two rabbit brothers, and a corresponding pair of guinea pig sisters. The basement apartment was inhabited by an older couple named Trudy and Bruce, and their scraggly senior cat Feather. Bruce was a solid, solitary man who spoke about as often as Feather the cat. Trudy was just as solid as Bruce, if not more, but their similarities ended there. Trudy was thoroughly uninteresting, relentlessly sociable, and the one person whose friendship I avoided like the plague. Trudy knew everyone in town, and she was a Geiger counter for gossip.

I couldn't stand the woman. In my head, I always called her Trudy the Snoop. Every time I wanted to leave the house, I had to tiptoe quietly over the floor, avoiding the squeaky areas in hopes of escaping her notice. It seemed that every time I opened the door, Trudy was right outside waiting to compliment me on my piano skills or ask me who I was dating or remark on how many times she heard our toilet flush throughout the day. She would joke that she always thought the ceiling would cave in on her head whenever she heard me dancing upstairs in my room. I found it unbearable, and I felt sorry for Feather the cat who eventually took to living outside and hiding when Trudy called her.

Feather was getting old and didn't get much peace. She was a skittish, bedraggled, flea-bitten thing. A few stripes still showed through her shaggy gray coat that was covered in mud and lumpy matts. Even though I pitied the aging creature, I couldn't help but respect her independence. Feather lived on her own terms, choosing solitude and uncertainty rather than a safe existence living indoors with that unbearable snoop. At night when everyone in the house was asleep, I sneak outside and make myself as comfortable as I could on the doorstep to see if Feather would creep by in the dark. Whenever I would spot her prowling under Trudy's red sedan, I would call to Feather softly and toss her some of Peter's cat treats. It took a long time for Feather to learn that I was a safe person. My strategy for winning her trust was to share some of my secrets with her. Feather heard me talk to the stars and ask the moon where my soulmate was, and she heard me sing quiet, lonely songs in the dark. One night after many chilly evenings by my doorstep, Feather got close enough for me to reach out and say hello. When you introduce yourself to a cat, you have to make a fist and hold it out in front of you as if it's a cat's head. That's how I met Feather properly. After that, we became friends. I would talk to Feather for hours sometimes, and I would leave her treats on my doorstep on the nights I didn't see her. I thought it was our secret, but one day Trudy caught me coming home from a solitary walk before I could dash into my house.

"Robyn," Trudy droned in her deep rumble, "I just wanted to tell you to stop leaving food out for Feather. She's getting so old, we're taking her to the vet tomorrow morning to have her put down."

I was horrified. Shadow was going to die the next morning unless I could convince Trudy to cancel that appointment with the vet. "Oh...Trudy," I began shakily, my heart already breaking. "Do you really have to do that? She's still pretty active. Couldn't you just wait–"

"No, no," the Snoop interrupted with a morose shake of her head. "We can't take care of her anymore, and she's in bad shape. It just has to be done."

That night as I lay in bed, I contemplated stealing Feather. All the time I knew I wasn't brave enough to try it. My mother wouldn't tolerate Feather's fleas for one minute, and I had to think of my own animals. The next day, I heard Trudy and Bruce take Feather away. I knew she was scared because I could hear her meowing from her crate, but I couldn't bring myself to look out the window. I hadn't been able to talk Trudy out of her stubborn resolve, but that wasn't even the worst part. I missed my last opportunity to save Feather because I was too scared to take a risk. Now Feather was stuck inside a cage in Trudy's red sedan with awful Trudy for company in her last moments. After that day, I tried to pretend Trudy didn't exist.

I remember those days as dark, cold, wet, and terribly lonely. After Feather was gone, I had to talk to the stars by myself and wonder when my soulmate would find me and rescue me from the cold, solitary woods. My job in Nashua didn't help matters. I was a dining room hostess and jackof-all-trades at a quick-service restaurant full of angry, impatient managers and customers. It was absolute hell. As lonely as home was, I found some solace in my quiet walks through the woods during my free time. I would walk for hours, and I wouldn't tell anyone where I was going. That way I could disappear to my most secret places to hide from the world and tempt fate.

Lyndeborough's only railroad track runs through the woods and leads to a rickety bridge over a ravine. The bridge is stable enough to support a person, but it doesn't hold still. When you step onto it, the whole structure groans and shifts slowly from side to side. There are wide spaces between the planks–not wide enough to fall through, but wide enough to prompt the imagination. It's not a footbridge, so there are no railings. If you take too many chances, it's a long way to the bottom of the ravine. I walked across that bridge a handful of times to see if my survival instinct was stronger than my death wish. The woods always found a way to tell me it wasn't my time.

One winter day after a horrible shift at work, I went on one of my secret walks down to Burton's Pond and ventured out onto the ice. Everything was dead quiet until I took my first step onto the frozen pond. *Cr-e-e-e-e-e-ak*. It made the most god-awful sound. Still, I kept walking, or rather shuffling over the ice. Slowly, gingerly, crouched forward with my hands out in front of me and took shallow breaths to make myself feel lighter. Every moment, something inside me shouted at me to go back. I ignored it.

The farther I got from the bank, the more relaxed I became. If I was here to meet my fate, I might as well enjoy my last moments. I looked up from the powdery floor of ice under my feet and looked around at the soft white beauty of the snow-covered woods and the colorless sky, and each wispy cloud my breath made as I silently made my way around the tiny island that stood on the middle of the pond like a scene from a snowglobe. I imagined how it would feel if the ice beneath my feet cracked and gave way, and what it would be like to plunge into the frigid water. I was so used to being cold and numb for most of my life that I wasn't entirely sure I was capable of freezing to death. And how deep was this pond, anyway? If it was too shallow, I'd have to force myself to sit there in the pond with my head above water while I waited for hypothermia to set in. After thinking about it for a while, I decided I didn't have the discipline. I trudged home and wondered if my soulmate would find me before my next work day. I found I needed Lyndeborough's stories and legends now more than ever to stave off despair.

One of my more beloved legends from Lyndeborough was Jerry–an old hermit who lived in a little old shack at the top of the hill by my house. Jerry was one of those local legends who seemed larger than life. According to a certain local gossip, Jerry did pretty well for himself in his younger days. Well enough to buy the large parcel of land he called Hilltop. In the short summers, he would drive to the city–probably Nashua–to find wayward youths loitering or causing trouble, and he would bring them back to Lyndeborough and let them run loose through the meadows and woods at Hilltop. He believed that the woods had the power to heal the body and soul. He had his tiny shack built and established his homestead there at the top of the hill on his "little piece of heaven" as he called it. Jerry had big ideas, but he lived simply and shared what he had, which was Hilltop. He wanted everyone to enjoy it. He would invite passersby to explore the woodland trails or fish down at Burton's pond or meet his animals, and on any given day you could find people hiking through the brush or running up and down the dirt road chasing after the cows whenever the bored bovines escaped their rickety enclosure. Yup, life was simple and sweet at Hilltop. The idyllic countryside was

Jerry's life's blood, and it was his wish to spend the rest of his life there. I didn't know that until after he died.

I only saw Jerry once. It was during the big ice storm of 2008. The power was out for nine days on our road, and one morning during the outage, my mother sent me up the hill to make sure the legendary Jerry was still alive in his shack. If he was alive, I was to ask him if he needed anything from the grocery store. My mother didn't give me any instructions in the case that he wasn't alive. I bundled up in my dirty featherdown parka, knitted cap, wool mittens, and old dirty snow boots I'd been wearing for ten winters since my early teens, and trudged up the dirt road through the woods to Jerry's house. It was eerie. The sun made the white sky glow, reflected in the glass of the ice-covered branches. Everything was completely encased in crystal-clear ice, and the road was dead silent without the hum of electricity or the usual sounds of wildlife bickering, munching, and scampering. I walked on the side of the road, punching my feet through the slippery layer of ice covering the mounds of snow. That's the way you have to walk when there's ice. Just stomp on it, one foot at a time.

When I finally reached the top of the hill out of breath and warm despite the wintery atmosphere, I regarded the snowy scene as I gathered my nerves. To my right, Jerry's herd of pet cattle were all gathered in their own dilapidated shed in the visible part of the cow field. To the left, Jerry's disheveled little shack stood, slightly crooked and dark with water damage. I really did not want to knock on that door. What if no one answered? Then what? See if the door was unlocked? Open it? What would I find inside? I have a terrible fear of dead things.

Cautiously, I approached the shack, trying to peer into the dirty windows to search for movement. I couldn't tell. I rapped on the door, gently as if the shack were a fragile shell that could collapse at any moment. Nothing happened. The horrible "what if" was upon me, and there was only one thing to do. I tried the handle and the door opened with a loud creak.

It was like walking into an oven. A tiny wood stove in the corner heated up the tiny cabin like a sauna. The single room had a homespun, cozy look which contrasted with the pungent stench emanating from the corner across from the wood stove. A sudden movement from the direction of the stench startled me, and I almost jumped out of my skin. In the corner, there was a narrow bed heaped with covers and a crochet afghan upon which a striped tabby cat was curled up comfortably. Propped up with pillows against the head of the bed was a very skinny old gentleman with a long, scraggly white beard streaked with gray. He had the look of a wild mountain man who had shriveled up into a little white raisin. His wide, popping eyes hovered over bony hands that trembled in a defensive position in front of his chest, and he looked as if he had just woken up from a dream about falling over a log and was recovering from the reflexive jolt. It all happened in a split second, and I realized all at once that he was both alive and every bit as startled as I was. More, probably! When you hole yourself up in the woods for decades until you're old and infirm, I imagine it's quite alarming when the door to your spindly little shack suddenly swings open and a strange young woman obliterates your peaceful solitude in one fell swoop.

"Oh! Uh....Jerry?" I greeted the bewildered white raisin, offering a nervous smile and an awkward wave as I shut the door behind me to keep in the heat. The wrinkles in Jerry's forehead smoothed out as his eyebrows slowly descended and resettled themselves over his eyes as he realized I wasn't here to ransack his home or murder him in his tiny bed. Still trembling, he gestured toward a spot between the wooden doorway and the dirty window. Following his brown fingernail, my eyes landed on the strangest-looking contraption on the wall next to me. The brown box had wires coming out of it leading to a rusty pair of headphones and what turned out to be a microphone. I suddenly remembered something Trudy had told me about Jerry— he was hard of hearing. This apparatus seemed to be a homemade hearing aid. I pointed at the device quizzically, and Jerry pointed and waved his directions until I gingerly took the headphones down from their hook and handed them to him. It took him a minute to put them on, and I realized his tremor was unrelated to his momentary shock at my entrance. Jerry was sick. His old age was only part of it. He feebly gestured to the microphone, and I picked up the dirty piece of machinery and attempted to use it.

"Hello, Jerry! My name is Robyn! I just wanted to see if you needed anything!" I shouted into the speaker. Jerry squinted and his head bobbed from side to side in confusion as the cat on his lap lazily regarded our activities from its bony bed. I was never good at projecting my voice, and my homespun enunciation didn't help. After a few tries, my voice only rose in pitch and Jerry only got more confused. I was confused, too. Jerry didn't exactly speak to me. He spoke in short, small grunts and murmurs, and his voice was too soft for me to pick out many syllables. Eventually, he peeled the huge headphones from his skull and handed them back to me. As I struggled to return the tentacles of the steampunk contraption to their holster without tangling up the cords too badly, Jerry slowly turned to a table at the side of his bed. Upon the table was a very old black typewriter with a piece of paper draped over the top, half full of faint black letters. I didn't know at the time that I had stumbled upon an artist at work. Jerry was writing his book on that old black typewriter. The old man couldn't even walk anymore, so he had made a cozy little nest for himself where he could look out the window at his beloved Hilltop and all the things that inspired him—the tumbledown stone wall, the dark leafy oaks and maples, the rocky dirt road where the occasional neighbor walked by, and the big open meadow where his cows meandered and grazed on the thick green grass in the brief, beautiful summers. I saw stacks of paper next to his bed, and the occasional loose pieces strewn about on the sparse furniture, on the floor, on the small desk next to the spindly bed. As I took in the state of it all, Jerry shakily took the piece of paper out of the typewriter and produced a pencil and a pair of scissors from somewhere. He put the paper down flat on the edge of the table and started scribbling at the bottom of the page. When he had finished writing, he picked up the paper in one hand and the scissors in the other, and brought them up close to his face. As I watched, he painstakingly cut the small strip of paper with the pencil scribbles from the rest of the sheet. Once he had accomplished his task, he held out the small strip of paper to me. I reached across his bed, took the jagged scrap of paper, and looked at it to see what Jerry had written.

milk 29¢
bread

That was all. I held a small piece of the legendary Jerry in my hand. Two words. Two essential items for survival in the winter woods. Bread and milk for the salt of the earth. I was honored to oblige.

I met the legendary Jerry just in time. He passed away the next year. If you read Jerry's obituary in the newspaper archives, they will say that Jerry died at Monadnock Community Hospital. But if you ask a Lyndeborougher, they'll tell you that Jerry fought the EMTs as they carried out his frail body on a stretcher. They'll tell you that Jerry got his final wish—he died on the doorstep of his little house on Hilltop. Maybe that's just the way we all want to remember

Jerry, but if you ask me, it's all true. Every word.

So far, it seemed that every local legend I had ever met was either tragic or infuriating. These characters prompted plenty of strong feelings and stark memories, but I was desperately looking for a happy ending–or at least a story that didn't end in death. In search of a lifeline, I threw myself into theatrical activities in a neighboring town. A town with *paved roads*, no less! I didn't realize then that I was starting to inch my way out of the woods.

One winter I auditioned for a community production of Seussical and was cast as a jungle animal. Our costumer, Sandy, was the perfect mix of warmth and practicality. Long-limbed with her blonde hair in a textured pixie cut, she moved quickly and got things done. She had a way of delivering bad news with an appropriate back-up plan that made you forget the bad news and approach the new plan with enthusiasm. When Sandy spoke, you listened. When the topic of self-costuming for the ensemble came up, Sandy had some specific rules for the jungle animals. "I don't want to see any animal ears! No tigers, no giraffes," Sandy announced firmly to the ensemble. "Make up an animal. It's Dr. Seuss!"

With no clear idea of how to proceed, I went to the party store and ended up leaving with a bright pink faux fur aviator hat, coordinating mesh gauntlets, and shaggy rainbow leg warmers. After raiding my closet for a rainbow leopard print top and yellow leggings, I attended the first costume check as a rainbow sasquatch creature I called the Squambat. Sandy was busy rejecting cat ear headbands and nixing black leotards, so her feedback was brief. "Robyn," she said matter-of-factly, "Nobody gets it but you." She gave me a brisk thumbs-up before turning her attention to a cast member wearing a Halloween panther costume. I must have been the happiest jungle animal at rehearsal in my fluffy rainbow ensemble. After that costume check, something inside me started to change.

Although it certainly wasn't necessary for my small background role in the play, I started to create a backstory for the Squambat. I decided her birthday should be different from mine. I chose March 9th, the date of the first costume check. Drawing inspiration from my mother's Scotch-Irish heritage, I imagined the Squambat as a puca or forest spirit whose purpose was to aid the farming community in my rural neighborhood. Like me, she would be naturally clumsy and a bit misguided when it came to helping out. It would be fun to tell Farmer John that it wasn't a rabbit that uprooted his garden, but a colorful sasquatch accepting her tribute in exchange for overwatering the tomatoes. The Squambat's vibrant appearance would be explained by her practice of stealing laundry off of clotheslines and putting together ridiculous outfits based on her observations of humans. The rainbow leopard print would be part of her strategy to blend in with her surroundings or pass for a human, depending on the situation. Eventually, the Squambat's given name emerged as Squidgin Marie Pennyfinder. I decided the Squambat would be an only child like me, raised exclusively by another, slightly less colorful creature called the Mombat–a traditionally reclusive sasquatch who discouraged the study of human behavior.

Gradually, I pieced together the Squambat's backstory as I reflected on my experience growing up in relative isolation with a poor understanding of how my own community functioned. The Squambat wasn't always like me. She was much more interesting and adventurous than I was. She was also irrepressibly optimistic, curious, and confident, contrasting with my depression and the feeling of being stuck in a haunted forest for the foreseeable future. The Squambat was an explorer, and she didn't need to be rescued. Every place was interesting to her, and if she didn't like where she was, she simply went somewhere else. Like the other local legends of Lyndeborough, the Squambat became my own source of comfort and inspiration that sustained my spirit through the dark times and cold weather. I didn't know that becoming the Squambat would lead to my escape from the woods.

I began to roam the neighborhood in full costume. I would bring my camera and film the Squambat scampering through Jerry's cowfield, crawling through Farmer John's corn, and hiding from approaching cars that looked like Trudy's red sedan. It started as a private project, but I soon found that the Squambat could not escape notice. My neighbors would spot her along the side of the road and stop to ask the inevitable question. "What's with the outfit?" I wasn't odd because of my family, or my hair, or my year-round tan anymore. I was becoming a new kind of oddity in town, and I liked it. If I kept it up, maybe someday the Squambat would become one of Lyndeborough's local legends, just like Jerry and Farmer John. And since I was the author of this legend, I could give it a happy ending.

It was the Squambat who helped me figure out that my soulmate wasn't in Lyndeborough, and it was because of the Squambat that I took my biggest chance since that winter day on Burton's Pond. When our landlords abruptly sold the little blue house, I packed up the Squambat and hopped on a plane to Portland, Oregon at the age of twenty-nine. It was as far away from Lyndeborough as I could possibly get without falling into the ocean. I loved it.

As a new story began, other chapters came to a close. My mother moved in with family to help my grandmother around the house and get her bearings as an empty nester. Trudy refused to leave the little blue house at first but eventually, she came around. She and Bruce live in one of Lyndeborough's neighboring towns, slightly closer to civilization. Jerry's family sold Hilltop, and someone built a yurt on the hill behind Jerry's shed. Maybe someone is writing a book up there. Who knows? As far as I know, you can still hike through the land and down to Burton's Pond. Go in the summer when it's nice. While you're there, you can probably find Farmer John who still takes care of Jerry's cows, including Peanut who has grown into a fine big fellow. As for me, I found my soulmate in Portland. We live together with our rescue dog and our little cat who listens to all my secrets. The Squambat is very happy in Portland.

Of course there was a reason I chose Portland to make a fresh start, but this story isn't about what I found in the city. It's about what I left in the woods. The beautiful oddities, the precious legends, the gravestones, the winter depression, and the first chapter of my greatest adventure. Leaving Lyndeborough was bittersweet, but when you grow up in the woods, you never really leave. The woods never really left me, either. All of my stories and lessons from Lyndeborough came with me to Oregon, and I'll keep them forever. Farmer John, Peanut, Jerry, Feather, Mom...even Trudy. They're still with me because they're all a part of me. And now they're a part of you, too.

REFRACTED

KIYANAH COOPER

I'm at work, on my way to clean the private event space on the upper floor. I work at a small movie theater on the outskirts of town, and there's a large forested area directly behind the building. That must be why there are so many cobwebs. The upper floor is accessible from two separate ways. The first and easiest way to get up there is the elevator, but the employees are usually forbidden to use it while working. The second way, is to use the old service ladder. There was once a service elevator, but that was deemed too unsafe for workers. So they tore it out and added a metal ladder. Like that's any better, it's probably far worse.

Opening the door slowly, I can feel a rush of cold air wrap around my limbs like a snake. It penetrates deep within my bones and makes me hesitate for a moment. There is no official light inside the shaft. The only minuscule amount of light that does manage to get through is the light of the event room itself. The room's lights are all gold but a layer of dust makes it silver coming down. It reminds me of moonlight, but it gives me no comfort and provides no beauty. Stepping up to the first rung of the ladder, I force my hand to grasp the rusted metal. Starting to climb, my body winces at the cold building up in my joints with every rung progression. It feels like my hands alone have aged ten years in thirty seconds. Spiders have penetrated this area too. I can feel the edges of spiderwebs. At times I can hear the fast scurrying of tiny spider paws as they patter across the walls. Hearing the filthy creatures scurry around me makes me shiver. I can't tell if I'm imagining the sensation of an arachnid's legs running down my spine and along my neck.

I'm trying not to rush my progression upwards. Last week Cindy, a young coworker of mine, tried to rush her way up but she squashed an unsuspecting centipede and freaked out. She fell from halfway up the ladder and sprained both ankles, her wrist, and her knee. My eyes scrunch up tightly, my jaw clenches, and slowly I make my way to the top. When the silvery light comes through the floorboards and starts to get brighter, I know I'm almost there. I reach my hand up and push gently against it. A small bit of dust falls onto the top of my head and sprinkles my eyelashes like indoor snow. I carefully move myself up the last few rungs of the ladder, pushing the small hatch of the floorboard up until it rests against the wall.

I feel like a meerkat, poking my head up out of the floor with squinted eyes, adjusting to the sudden light of the room after my time in the shaft. I hoist myself out of the hole like I'm getting out of a pool. I always do the awkward sit and shimmy, then turn and stand. It just feels safer than trying to raise my whole leg over the edge all at once. As I'm standing up, I'm trying to shake off the dust back down into the hole so as not to make any more mess to clean. I usually start my cleaning by dusting the inside of the hatch. No one else ever does. Closing the hatch gently, I stand to open the cleaning pantry, which is very well hidden. The door to the pantry is camouflaged inside a very large abstract red painting. It looks like a city at night to me, but I've heard others say it looks like red rain. The door handle is that of a pullout semicircle and it lays perfectly flat inside the painting when not in use. It is hidden inside a shadow in the painting, and you would never find the handle unless someone told you where it was.

Inside the little space is a broom, duster, cleaning spray, paper towels, a few microfiber cloths, and tableware. Along with a few bus bins. I take the duster, the broom, the spray, and a microfiber cloth from the pantry. I stand there for a moment taking in the magnificent details of the room. I know I should be cleaning, but I just can't help but scan the room from right to left, examining every ornate detail.

A very long mahogany table is visible on the right-hand side of the space. The chairs look like thrones, all with pointed wooden backs, intricately carved armrests, and poofy deep red velvet cushions. Along the wall, a booth bench with deep red leather seats hugs one long side of the table. A red table runner and a full bouquet of roses catch my eye from the tabletop. Right across from me is the old elevator with black doors and gold details. The inside of the elevator is luxurious, but the employees are only allowed to use it when carrying bus tubs.

Two large windows stand on either side, each framed by large red curtains with gold fringe along the edges and bottoms. The curtains are pulled up at the sides to reveal the view. The view in question is simply midsections of trees regressing quickly backward in the mist from the forest behind the building. A tall lamp with a red shade and gold fringe lights the right side of the elevator. On the left-hand side of the room is a grand golden fireplace with a hand-carved solid gold mantle. The pillars holding up the mantle are shaped like beautiful young women in long flowy dresses. Atop the mantle is an old gold clock with a glass dome over the top, a mid-sized antique hourglass, and an old globe. Above this is a very old ornate gold mirror. It's rather beautiful, in a haunting sort of way. My manager told me in secret during one of my lunch breaks that it belonged to the owner's wife a long time ago. The owner never talks about her and no one knows why he chose to put the mirror in the event room.

I rather enjoy cleaning this room. It smells like cedar and whisky and expensive cigars. It's got a feeling of exclusivity and power to it that the rest of the theater just doesn't have. It has all of the elements of my childhood home. It makes me feel welcome and safe but still a little on edge. It feels like knowing you've done something wrong and you've gotten away with it, but someone's onto you. Like knowing there's no proof and in that way, nothing bad can happen to you.

I've started dusting the inside of the hatch. Try as I might, I can't stop myself from thinking about Cindy. I look down and imagine her panic as she plummets down toward the cold ground. Her hair flowing upward as she falls. I can see how her face contorts with horror, and I can hear her high-pitched screech while I'm cleaning the edges of the floorboards where the hatch lays. Closing the newly cleaned hatch, I force the image of Cindy's contorted body out of my mind.

I have to grab a chair from the grand table because I'm too short to reach the top of the mantle on my own. With my shoes removed, my feet step up onto the soft cushion of the throne-like chair, after taking the duster and spray in one hand to my workspace. I then begin dusting the glass over the gold clock, looking at the mirror in the corner of my eye while cleaning, and suddenly my whole being is gripped by fear and shock. My eyes are frozen on the base of the clock in the glass but I force my vision to track the mirror as hard as I can.

There is the silhouette of a man standing in the mirror, or maybe a shadow. The surface of the mirror looks like sea glass. It's foggy, forcing me to try to focus my eyes more firmly on the figure, and it makes everything so non-concrete. Some features I can make out, but they're all wrong. His nose looks like a lightning bolt, his eyes are in different places, and his mouth seems to be crooked on his face. I stand frozen, staring at the figure, afraid to blink or breathe. He is very tall. His head almost touches the top of the gold frame of the mirror, and he seems to be looking straight down his nose into me.

My body starts to move on its own. The duster on the ledge of the mantle makes a small clinking noise, though I'm being as silent as possible, still holding my breath. I can't stop myself from moving closer to the glass. My hands seem to move on their own up to it. My brain manages to take over again for a moment, and my hands are left only inches away from the smooth foggy surface in front of me. The figure appears to be breathing, and I can hear a muffled sound of panting coming out. Or maybe it's a muttering. The sound is struggling to get to me in a way I can only describe as hearing your neighbor through the wall of your apartment. My fingertips feel a chill radiating off of the glass's silky surface. It traps me there, penetrating my palms with its chilly air.

The figure is moving more now. I can feel the hairs on the back of my neck stand up. The edges of my vision go black with fear. It appears to be examining me. Taking in my shape, my features, and my body. I can't pull my arms back. The figure moves its hands to the glass, with fingertips pressed gently on the surface. It seemed like the figure was waiting for me. I try my best to pull my hands away from the milky mirror, but my palms press flat against it anyway.

The cold makes the glass stick to me, and the figure in the mirror makes it all the colder to push against. To my shock and horror, my hands slip through the mirror, and I fear that the figure will pull me into its abyss and drown me there. I've realized that the mirror will not let me go and that there is no point in wasting my energy trying to fight it. If I become trapped in the mirror with the deformed figure,

I'll need my strength. I close my eyes, turn my head down, and push deeper into the glass.

*

My body bursts upright, almost shaking with fear. I look around and see only darkness for a moment. Slowly, my vision starts to return to me. A feeling of cold sweat runs down my brow, and my armpits and back are drenched. My eyes have started to adjust to the dark room but I can't make heads or tails of it. It all looks upside down, and nothing seems familiar. I wonder for a moment how much time has passed. I wonder what's happened in that time. Was I kidnapped? No. I couldn't have been. Could I? *No.*

Looking down, I notice blankets and sheets over my legs. Looking over my shoulder I find a multitude of familiar pillows. Quickly I looked around the rest of the room more closely. This is my room in my apartment. My little Cheshire cat clock shows 6:53 am. Must have been a nightmare. I inhale deeply and release my breath slowly, yet my whole body shivers as my heart races. I try to control my breathing, forcing the air to come in through my nose and out through my mouth until dizziness sets in.

My alarm is set for seven A.M. so I can get ready to go to work. This is the sixth time since I started this job that I've had this nightmare. The glass always traps me, but the figure never gets ahold of me. I worry that this is not a coincidence. I've heard that dreams can tell you things. It could be that there is someone at work who doesn't wish me well. Or maybe the mirror and the distorted figure is a metaphor for living a life that isn't true to myself. Either option displeases me.

Grabbing my keys and my bag, I start out the door while I savor the last bite of my bagel. My hair is piled up in a bun on top of my head, and it looks messy and cute. There are lots of loose strands that frame my face. Pressing the button for the elevator, I can't help but comb through all I can remember of the nightmare I've been having. How long is this going to plague my sleep? Will the dreams only stop if I quit my job? Will this happen with my other jobs? Am I really overthinking fictional events in my head on the way to work? I get into the elevator, and allow it to carry me down through the floors.

The elevator makes many stops. People get in, and people get out. Down and down we go. None of this particularly interests me. There is an attractive young man who got in the elevator a couple of floors ago, but he doesn't seem to notice me. I pretend not to notice him but steal a few glances in his direction anyway. When we reach the first floor, the young man ambles out of the elevator, and I walk confidently by. Maybe he will smell my expensive perfume, notice my confidence and my cute hair, and come talk to me. He does no such thing. He mutters to himself as I walk by, but he was muttering on the elevator too, so I think nothing of it.

This is a small apartment near the heart of downtown, and it's fairly busy most of the time. Today is not unusual as far as the general population is concerned. No more or less people than every other day. Luckily for me, this means that the bus stop just down the block is not crowded. So I will be able to get coffee at the Starbucks across the street and sit while waiting for the bus.

With drink in hand I walk back toward the bus stop. Blowing through the straw hole of my drink, I look up and see that the young man from the elevator is standing at the bus stop. He is still muttering, but I pay no mind and sit down on the bench next to him. We board the bus one after the other, along with an older couple and a few schoolgirls clearly cutting class. Three stops go by. Then five, and then eight. Nearly everyone is off the bus now, but the man is still there and muttering to himself.

I get off the bus, and so does the man. He follows

behind me, still muttering to himself. The theater is only a short walk from the bus stop, but it's cold this morning. I feel like I've been walking for miles. Still having quite a bit of coffee left, I use it to warm my hands. The theater is visible now. It doesn't look very busy, which is odd for a Saturday morning.

As soon as I come in, I see Jess chewing her bubblegum while on her phone at the empty concessions counter, leaning on the wall. When she sees me, she snaps to attention. I laugh and look around the front room. There is no one here.

"Girl! I thought you were a customer!" She says to me. She must have noticed that I was confused about why no one was there because she said, "Two people came, so I guess that's something." She stops and looks at the door. "Welcome in sir! What can I do for you?" She says with a smile in her best customer service voice.

When I look at the door, I see the man from before entering the theater. He mutters to himself, paying her no mind, and walks straight through the door across from the concessions stand. That's the door that leads to the stairs and the basement office with the break room. That's also where the owner stays all day while he works. I tell Jess about my morning journey and the strange man muttering at my heels the whole time.

"Dang. I wonder what he's here for. He didn't even hesitate," Jess says as she watches me clock in and throw away my empty coffee cup. I give her a small nod in return and start to wonder what he could be doing downstairs.

"Do you think I should go down there and see what's going on?" I'm looking at the door, but I already know she will tell me not to worry about it.

"No. The owner can handle himself. But if you want something to do, I left a perfectly messy bathroom for you to clean." She beams at me, and I give her a look as I head to the cleaning closet. Then to the women's bathroom. Jess always leaves me little surprise tasks for when I get to work. She says it makes me look more productive, but I know she just doesn't want to do it.

When I've finished cleaning the bathroom, I head back to the concessions counter where Jess is making popcorn for an elderly couple we see a lot. She smiles as they walk out and then sweeps the lobby while I restock the cups and straws. Plus whatever else we need.

"Oh, Daphne, I almost forgot! The owner came up and said you should clean the event room. I already cleaned the theater from the event this morning and I can handle the front by myself for a bit." She rushes off before I can ask about the young man.

The ladder is just as bad as how I dreamt it. Pushing open the hatch, the dust falls just like it did in my dream. Everything seems perfectly normal until I see the young man standing before the mantle. He is looking into the glass and pressing his palm against it, still muttering. For a moment, I'm so surprised by his presence that I almost step backward and fall into the shaft. My foot catches on the hatch, and it slams shut with a very loud bang. The young man, startled, looks right at me for the first time.

"Who are you? Did my dad send you up here to clean?" He speaks to me completely normally. He doesn't say anything else but waits patiently for me to respond. He is quite handsome. He has dark skin, green eyes, and curly brown hair. He wears a loosely fitted long-sleeved shirt with long dress pants and a black belt. His shirt is a nice shade of forest green that makes him stand out nicely from the rest of the room. It takes me a moment to respond to him.

"I'm Daphne. I was sent to clean. Who are you?" I won't stand and stare at him in anticipation of a response. Instead, I gather the cleaning supplies from the pantry. He tells me his name is Nick and he is the owner's son. That would explain why he wasted no time going downstairs. I still can't help but wonder why he has his hand pressed against the glass of what must be his mother's mirror. Why would he leave fingerprints all over it?

"I came to ask my father to give me my mother's old mirror. It was a long shot considering its history, but it was worth a try." I give him a confused look while dusting the hatch. "Has my father really not said anything about it?" I shake my head, and he laughs. "My father is under the impression that my mother's spirit lives inside this mirror. She and my father had a strained relationship after he started seeing another woman. She didn't really love him. Their relationship was just a matter of reputation for her. He says that things started to happen after she died. Wherever the mirror was in the house, something close by would always break. He moved the mirror many times, but it was only when he moved it here that things stopped breaking."

I start to wonder why he's telling me all of this. Isn't this a bit too much information to be telling a stranger? To be fair, I have wondered why he would leave such a pretty mirror in his place of work rather than at his house. Never would I believe anything he said about his mother's spirit being in the mirror if it wasn't for the dreams I've been having recently.

"I always thought my father was losing his mind. Maybe it was all just a coincidence. Maybe his cat was knocking things over. He was adamant that my mother was getting back at him for his cheating. It would serve him right, but I never believed it until a few weeks ago when I started having strange dreams about the mirror. I want to keep it in my apartment for a while so I can put it to the test. Will you help me steal it?" He looks at me with a sparkle in his eye like a child waiting to find out if they can have a cookie.

My response comes before the last line of what he said fully registers with me. "Wait, you've had strange dreams about the mirror too?" The words are out before I can think about it. His face changes to confusion

"You've been dreaming about my mother's mirror?"

"Hold on a second. Did you just ask me to help you steal your own mother's mirror from your father and the owner of my place of work?" I look at him with the most "Why on earth would I do that, or even consider it?" look.

"We can get back to that. What have you been dreaming about that involves my mother's mirror?" He is standing in front of me now, looking down at me expectantly. I have no intention of telling him anything until he tells me something first. I put my hands on my hips and turn my nose up. He rolls his eyes and sighs before speaking.

"My father always thought that my mother wanted him to see her in the mirror and feel guilty about what he did to her. I think she wants me to see her in the mirror instead. It feels like she's trying to guide me to something, but I can't understand it. In my dreams, she guides me here to this mirror and tells me to look inside. When I do, I see the figure of a young woman." My face goes white. I also saw a figure in the mirror in my dreams. Why would a woman I've never met before be forcing me to dream about her son?

"She tells me that if I find the mirror I'll find this person, but when I look in the mirror the face is all contorted. Nothing is in the right spot. It's like her message was being refracted in my dream, and so nothing was matching up right. I thought that if I looked into the mirror in person, the face would be clear. I don't see anything here except you and..." He trails off.

I can tell he's thinking about his mother's message. Temptation builds in me to turn right around and go back down the ladder. I don't. Firstly, because he and I are having the same dream about the same mirror, and we each see a distorted figure. Plus I can't see any way that this could be a coincidence. Second, because I don't want to lose my job for walking out and not cleaning the event room like I was specifically asked to. Also, partly because my curiosity is killing me.

He has begun to mumble again. I hate the way he is looking so closely at me. The last couple of nights have been rough, I don't want this guy to pick apart my eye bags and compare them to his mystery figure. So I walk around him and pull a chair up to the mantle so I'll be tall enough to clean his handprint off the glass. I climb up on the chair, nearly hitting my head on the edge of the mantle and stand up.

"Be careful! You'll break something." He walks over while I'm wiping the fingerprints and grabs the mirror's frame. "Let me take that down for you. It'll be much easier to clean off the wall."

"No! It's such a hassle to get it straight again, don't bring it down!" Too late. He is already lifting it off the nail in the wall, and I'm trying my best to push the top back and get the hook back on the nail. The mirror falls, and I gasp.

"Shit!" Nick yells. He tries to catch it, but it slips from his fingers. It hits the cushion of the chair I'm standing on and bounces off onto the floor. We are both left staring at the mirror for a moment. There was no shattering of glass, and we both sigh in relief. He goes and picks up the mirror, looking at both sides. He frowns at it and for a split second, I think it must have cracked. He flips the mirror around so the glass is away from him and sets it gently on the table.

"What's wrong with it? Did it crack?" sliding off of the chair I'm rushing to look at the damage. There is no crack in the mirror at all. Instead, a small piece of paper with a note written in perfect cursive. It reads, "I hope you find who you're looking for, like I never could. I love you, Nick." I'm stunned. His theory about his mom leaving the mirror for him and not his father was correct.

He leaves the note where it is and flips the mirror over. Then takes the cleaning supplies from me and wipes away the mark he made on the surface. Finally, he hangs the mirror back in its place. His eyes peer into my eyes and he says, "I think my mom likes you. Can I give you my number and we can get dinner sometime?"

It's been two years since the mirror fiasco, and Nick and I are engaged to be married. When we told the story at our engagement party, Nick's father decided to give us the mirror. I haven't had a nightmare since, and nothing ever breaks in our home.

MURDER SHE CROAKED

JACKLYN-DIANA DUREKE

CONTENT WARNINGS:
Murder, drug use, abuse

"I should have never killed her," Pépé admitted to his journal during a foggy ghostly night, his mind shaking with regret and fear. He sat alone on the cliffs overlooking the churning lake, his heart heavy with the weight of the actions he had committed. The waves billowed in a symphony of fluid motion, the white foam like a mesmerizing display of what the earth created in mounds. He could almost see her there, beckoning him with her eyes that had once twinked like a star in the sky as the moon cast an eerie glow over him. Vanessa was the love of his life; their hearts were intertwined like ivy on an ancient castle wall. They seemed to always find their way back to each other every other couple of months, no matter how many times they broke up. Their love story had once been filled with passion, love, and tenderness until a dramatic mistake was made when Pépé ended Vanessa's life.

Pépé's days have been consumed by grief and guilt since that horrible night. After the murder, he struggled to get up and get ready for work. He no longer had Vanessa there to wake him up. "Pépé, honey, get up. You gotta start getting ready for work, my love," she would call to him.

Vanessa made his breakfast and lunch every morning. Pépé worked as an architect manager for a construction company, which did quite a number on Pépé's body. He started taking opiates to help stop his muscles from the pain after a horrific work accident. A forklift sliced through his abdomen one day after a highly anxious worker who was underqualified for the job hit Pépé. Pépé had gone for counseling in church, and the dreams were always recurring—the same scene.

June 8th, 2011

After a stressful day of work, Pepé made his daily stop at Mama Frank's corner shop for his usual 24-four-pack of Heineken. By the time he got home, Pepe was halfway through his sixth bottle. Vanessa scurried to greet and embrace him upon his arrival but recoiled at the stench of his breath.

"Nuh uh, not this," she nagged, shaking her head. "Drinking again?" Pépé brushed past her, pack in hand, rolling his eyes in response.

"We've talked about this before," Vanessa pressed. "I don't appreciate you coming home like this—"

"—Well, if you had the day that I did, you'd want to drink too," Pépé jabbed, cutting her off. "I've had a long day, I don't want to be stressed at home too."

"Well, if that's the case, then I'm out," she replied.

"Yeah, right," Pépé thought. Yet another bluff. This was just a part of their routine. Yeah, they'd fight but they'd always start the next day like nothing happened. Beer still in hand, Pépé grabbed his dinner, settled on the couch, and turned on the TV. However, unbeknownst to Pépé, for once Vanessa meant business. The audio of the hit show "Shameless" muted her movements as she swiftly packed her things. Pépé didn't notice until he felt a chilly drift from the opening door.

"This way neither of us will be stressed at home" Vanessa snided.

Pépé rushed to convince her to stay, grabbing her wrists and forcing her back inside.

"Let go of me" Vanessa winced "You're hurting me Pépé ." She deliberately drove her elbow into his side, sending him stumbling back and losing his footing. Usually he turned the other cheek at her physical jabs. He never took them personally as he knew it was out of her frustration. That was before Vanessa uttered:

"Look at you" she snided, making sure to get a whole look of him, "You're a piece of shit business owner, a piece of shit son, a horrible provider, and now we can add a piece of shit husband to the list, too."

Pépé's head went black. Their abusive back and forth seemed to never end. But blood gushing out from Vanessa's head finally brought him back. As Pépé glanced at Vanessa, he realized she was immobile. The blood gushing from her head trickled from glass shards in her thick eyebrows, ruining her beautiful face. In his shock, the Heineken bottle slipped from his grip, shattering against their hardwood floors.

The number of times he went to church to repent couldn't save him. Vanessa's name seemed to echo in every shadow and whisper, a haunting reminder etched with the precision of a master sculptor. Every time he stepped outside, the world conspired to remind him of his actions in vivid, unforgiving detail. The elongated ghost cast by the street lamps reached out to him, as if accusing fingers pointed at every move he made, every corner he turned the ghost stretched towards him. Even the tiniest whisper in the wind carried a sliver of her name, an ephemeral wisp that clung to his conscience like a relentless specter. The world had become a tapestry woven with guilt, and he, its unwilling captive, had become ensnared in the chilling embrace of his past. Months passed, and as Vanessa's death anniversary approached, Pépé's agony grew worse. He started to hear her voice, a soft, ethereal whisper on the wind, calling his name in a beseeching plea for forgiveness. She scratched his face and skin, trying to save herself. Blood gushing down from her head, Pépé had pushed her back, and she fell and hit her head on the rock behind him. Telling him to stop, "Pépé, you're hurting me, my love. I'm so sorry," said Vanessa as she scooched back quickly, moving away from him. The ghost of her face appeared in the corners of his vision, her eyes sad and longing, full of tears, her form translucent and luminous against the raging storm.

Pépé felt a chilling presence beside him one stormy night as he stood on the same cliff where his beloved Vanessa had met her tragic end. Though he couldn't touch her, he could feel the warmth of her love and forgiveness emanating from her ghostly form. His heart ached with remorse as he begged her forgiveness, tears streaming down his cheeks. "Vanessa, I was inebriated. That wasn't me," Pépé screamed out to the ghostly figure of Vanessa.

January 2nd, 2013

The New Year just passed but Pepé wanted to, no, he needed to celebrate it with his boys. Yesterday was a disaster for Vanessa and him. Her family found out about the abuse.

Pépé's laughter became increasingly erratic as the night went on, and even his friends were unable to understand the darkness in his eyes. In the swirling mist of intoxication, the group's conversations became jumbled and the words lost their meaning.

"Take it easy, Pépé, my boy," said Sueno, a worried friend whose voice sounded like a faraway wail.

"Dude, are you seeing things again?" Sueno yelled into

his face.

Pépé's laughter became louder as the evening wore on, and the warmth of companionship blended with the intoxicating effects of alcohol.

The moment Pépé stepped into his apartment, the atmosphere became stuffy and heavy with a funk. His girlfriend Vanessa was waiting for him in the poorly lit living room, a haunting look of worry on her face.

As Pépé staggered into the apartment, reeking of alcohol, his laughter now tinged with aggression, despite Vanessa's best efforts to help. The flickering candlelight created strange shapes on the walls in the engulfing silence that followed.

Something broke inside Pépé as soon as his eyes locked with Vanessa's. It appeared as though evil spirits were inhabiting the room, causing it to twist and deform.

"Are you alright, Pépé? How did it go?" Vanessa inquired with a sincere worry in her voice.

"I'm alright! Just had a great time hanging out with the guys. Why do you always take things so seriously?" Pépé slurred, moving unsteady as he talked.

"Just checking in to make sure you're okay." With growing concern, Vanessa insisted, "You seem really drunk."

"Quit being such a buzzkill, alright? I'm good." Pépé pushed her away with a force that took her by surprise as his tone became dismissive.

With a look of confusion mixed with hurt, Vanessa staggered backward. "This isn't like you. Why is this happening?"

Pépé's anger increased and his mood grew even darker. The apartment turned into a battlefield for a confrontation that neither of them anticipated.

"Why must you bother me so much? You spoil everything so much that I can't even enjoy myself!" Pepé became even more enraged, his words laced with poison.

"Pépé, I just need to understand what happened to you." Vanessa begged, her attempts at reason met with a violent storm, "You're spooking me."

Alcohol-fueled rage consumed Pépé, who then unleashed a blackout-fueled fury that brought the confrontation to a terrifying crescendo. Unknowingly, Vanessa was the victim of the chaos of the night because she was caught in the maelstrom.

The sounds of a struggle and Vanessa's cries reverberated through the apartment, which had previously been filled with laughter and hope. This violent outburst permanently changed the trajectory of their relationship by leaving deeper scars rather than the superficial wounds from before.

The wind carried away their pain and anger in that haunted moment, leaving only love and forgiveness in its wake. Vanessa's ghostly figure faded away, and Pépé thought he felt the weight of his actions lift off his shoulders. Vanessa's memory remained in his heart, a constant reminder of the frailty of love and the consequences of unchecked rage. He kept vowing to God and his new girlfriend Josefina, that he would live a life of kindness and compassion, cherishing the haunting love that had once bound them and now served as a beacon of hope in his life that he was still able to live.

Vanessa was a 23-year-old Virgo, who was full of life and had a spicy mouth on her. Loved going out to parties and trying new foods. Just fresh out of college, living outside of downtown Houston in an apartment with Pépé. She graduated from the University of Houston with a degree in Finance and Latin American Studies. Her parents were immigrants from Mexico, the city of Michoacán, and she was the baby of the family—the last child of 3 with two older brothers, Jose and Feliz, who are Irish twins. From her mother, she learned Brujeria, known as witch culture. She practiced it to get anything she wanted, but when someone did her wrong, she'd pray hell onto them. The dark craft is always her last resort when someone falls into a bad situation.

She met Pépé, at a hazy Halloween party her freshman year on October 31, 1999, with her new friends Josefina and Guadalupe at a college party their freshman year.

That night she experimented with drinking for the first time, jungle juice is what they called it. That deep red liquid that smells rancid!

" Oh, what is this? Colored rubbing alcohol?" said Vanessa.

"Girl, just take a sip. We will be fine," yelled Josefina and Guadalupe over loud music.

They continued to dance and party that night. Vanessa took a breather and sat down on a worn-down futon in the living room area. She was over it. The party was fun but she was ready to go to bed. She wanted to finish any last-minute homework she had before Monday. She sobered up about a half hour ago. She finally felt back to herself.

"Yo, what's ya name?" said a mystery man who Vanessa did not know nor had seen before.

"Uhmm my name's Vanessa. And you?" Vaness yelled into his ear. The music was so loud they moved closer to each other to hear one another.

Vanessa noticed how good he smelled. It gave her butterflies in her belly yet, to her butterflies were a sign of danger in brujera culture. She disregarded them.

"Pépé." the man simply said.

They shook hands softly. Pépé smiled. "You are beautiful. Why come? I've never seen you around here." said Pepe.

"This is my first year here. That's why." Vanessa said with sass.

"Play hard to get Vanessa," she softly mumbled to

herself.

"Oh aight." Pépé liked her attitude, something inside him made him want her even more.

January 3rd, 2013

Every time she was upset, Vanessa went to her favorite cliff 2 hours out of Houston to Lake Houston Wilderness Park. She has been trying to work on their relationship lately. Even with her self-love, all this pain is killing her. After all the abuse and toxicity, Vanessa wanted to give it another go. After each fight, Vanessa leaves their apartment to give Pepe space. At least, that's what her mother always said to do, *"Mija leave, it's not your fault. La Bruja said he is fighting an evil spirit. When the time comes both of you will be fine."* Vanessa sat on the bench crying. She must pray to La Bruja for change. Life has been too stagnant for the last decade now.

Pépé knew there was only one place that Vanessa could be. He took that drive out to the park. Where was she? The evil spirits inside him were itching. They chanted to him, *"HURT HER, KILL HER!"* Pépé started scratching himself to stay calm, leaving red marks all over himself. "She thinks she can leave me. Oh, I'll show you," he yelled in the car. Just as he pulled up it started raining. The sky above, covered in dark gray hues that were menacing, loomed like a ghostly painting, whispering secrets from unseen specters carried by the wind.

Pépé cornered Vanessa on the lonely cliff, the tension in the air compounded by the distant rumble of thunder that mirrored his inner turmoil. Pépé's eyes, which had been warm and with love for her, glowed with an unholy fury as the dark clouds overhead churned and the wind whispered dark secrets.

"Vanessa, are you leaving me? Do you really believe that?" With a voice like a poisonous snake, Pépé's voice was warped by the evil spirit that was eating him.

With a terrified expression on her face, Vanessa begged Pépé to change the situation. "I simply need more time."

The sinful force that had laid dormant within Pépé, now awakened, rising to power, provoking him with alarming suggestions, carrying a ghostly symphony of evil spirits' whispers. He kept asking Vanessa questions until his sanity faltered.

"You're lying!" Pépé erupted in a fury, as sheets of rain fell onto their faces, washing away their tears that mixed with the growing violence between both of them. Vanessa backed away, with blood running down her head from the previous fall, at the edge of the cliff, a delicate line separating her life from an executing horror below it.

Pépé felt the evil spirit inside him urging him to let out his anger. With his bare hands, swirled by the darkness within, he pressed hard against Vanessa's chest in an instant. She fell into the toiling lake, her screams and cries echoing with the wind like an orchestral piece of madness. He watched her body bounce off of the cliff's rocks, landing near the lake's edge. The storm gave a roaring approval, as though the unholy deed was witnessed by nature itself. Pépé rose from the edge, his hands trembling with Vanessa's blood smeared on them, the evil spirits now freed into the middle of the storm. The rain had begun to erase any proof of the heinous deed he had done, revealing only the eerie remnants of a love turned gruesome tragedy.

The storm continued, the cliffside turning into a haunting portrayal of a love lost to the darkness within a troubled man, as the wind carried the sinister laughter that echoed inside of Pépé's plagued soul. The rain kept tumbling down, eroding the last fragments of humanity from a man now consumed by the evil spirits that found a home in the recesses of his broken psyche.

THE MARSHLANDS

RILEY REYNOLDS

His wrought iron lantern
His aged crooked staff
Lighting the marshlands below...

Be careful, be weary
Best not cross his path
Lest ye find yourself buried...

Buried within,
The marshlands below...

May 11th, 1651 - The Lantern Man

Men speak of ghostly lights guiding the foolish and ill-witted to a shallow grave. I had always regarded these tales as simple fiction. Never did I imagine that I would write to you, dear reader, a warning of my own.

Another cold night keeping watch over the northmost point of the fenlands. I remember the moonlight slowly glinting in as the clouds rolled overhead. The wind chilled my bones as my feet sunk into the soft wet earth. Despite the best attempts of the wind to warn me, I was capable of lighting a flame within my small hold. Oh dear reader, how I regret such action now. The fire warmed my bones, but it called forth something far more sinister than I could have foreseen.

Through a misty pane of my old crooked window, I saw a small flame alight in the marshlands, could not have been further than sixty paces. I questioned to myself who would dare travel through the bog at this hour? I left my den with curiosity, seeing to approach this stranger. Dear reader, how horrible a decision that was. I stepped out into the cold of the swamp and called out into the darkness.

"Hail fellow, identify yourself!" Only the hushed sounds of the mire echoed back.

Slowly, the light grew closer. As it did my eyes began to distinguish a thin wooden quarterstaff. Latched to the end of it was an iron lantern that swung like a bell tolling death. I could not see the figure that held it through the reeds, but I watched it gather closer still. Feeling unease, I readied an old flintlock my father had passed on to me subsequent to his death. Had I known what had killed him, I should have ran right then, but curious and without foreknowledge, I stayed put and waited for the man's approach.

As he stepped out from the reeds, I raised my gun. "Halt! Declare thyself before I fire!"

The man kept pace towards me. As I lifted my finger ready to fire, I saw the creature's face. A mangled cacophony of peat, burlap, and reeds, something that stood against God now stood before me. I fired against it, watching the lead ball pierce the creature's side. It did not even break its stride, as it kept a forward path through the bog. I fired twice more upon it as it slowly approached. Whilst I loaded my fourth and last shot, I began to run. Yet, as I did, the thick mud clung to my feet, holding me back as I struggled to make my longest stride.

When it reached striking distance, it swung with its staff. I fell to the ground, yet did not manage to escape the blow, taking a sharp hit to the head. Looking up, I saw its body marked by my shots, yet still seemingly unharmed. My vision darkened as I struggled in the muck, trying my hardest to escape. My arms and legs grew heavy as I felt my body succumb to the soft mud. I closed my eyes and accepted my fate as the cold water wrapped around my shaking body.

The next morning I awoke to the sun bearing down upon me, for I had lived to see another day. Still half-buried within the bog, I thanked God and the spirits of the fens for sparing this miserable soul of a horrible fate. However, I am afraid I had offered my thanks too soon.

I crawled forward, heaving myself from the mire. Struggling to stand. I felt my limbs burning from exhaustion. Despite my latent panic and fear, I took at least a quarter of an hour to rest and gather my thoughts of the night prior. Any sane man would refute what I had witnessed, but no man would remain sane after seeing such a being. Visions of its figure still plagued my mind, the scent of the bog only aiding in my anxiety.

Still worn and ragged, I dragged my heavy legs toward my hold. While my body demanded rest, I forced myself to clean off the muck from myself before lighting a fire. My soiled clothes remained outside in a sodden heap, myself in no better condition. No work would be done that day, for I spent it resting both body and soul. Yet my mind was still restless. I braced my windows shut and placed a large cabinet behind the door. After which, I prayed to God for my safety and to the spirits that they may remain clear of my den this night. I closed my eyes to rest, as the pale moonlight trickled in through my window.

The noise came before anything else. With the rapping of wood and metal against my door, the cabinet shook but held firmly. I reached for my gun, finding it missing from its original resting place at the foot of my bed. First came panic, then dread upon realizing I had left it among the marsh the previous morning. I crept slowly from my bed towards the window. Peering through the bracings, I looked out into the mire into complete and utter darkness save for the light of a familiar lantern. I saw the figure turn to face me with what I can only assume to be a smile lurking across its face. While its body sagged in the marsh, its gaze held firm, I felt it pierce my very being. And then, nothing.

With a start, I awoke upright, my legs half-buried in the bog. The sun shone down upon me, begging me to wake. I had awoken in the marshlands with no memory as to my arrival. Had I not found myself outdoors, I would believe it to be only but a nightmare. To my luck, I had woken only a few paces from my hold. As I made my way inside, the sun proudly shone through the same window I had stared through but moments ago in a dream. Lifting myself out of the bog, I found parts of my body caked in dried muck, sticking to my garb as I removed myself from it. Still worried from the visions that had plagued my mind in the night, I opened the door and looked out across the marsh. No signs or marks that someone or something had been here, so I dismissed it as merely a vivid construction of the mind. I would have gone to fetch my gun right then had it not been for the cold winds that blew across my unguarded flesh.

I washed my clothes before anything else. stained but now clean, I hung them to dry. Next came the bedding and, finally, myself. I scrubbed violently against the marks of the bog that tainted my very being. As I scrubbed, I felt the lye begin to burn at my skin, and soon I resigned myself to the marks. I believed them to rub off in a matter of days. You will soon know, dear reader, how wrong I was. It would seem I would go through most of my soap that day.

A matter of hours later, I took my now dry clothes and readied myself to retrieve my gun. Stepping out I felt the wind, glad for the protection of my newly cleaned garments. Keeping a watchful eye to the reeds around me, I walked through the marsh in search of my gun. Each step was carefully followed by a gaze of my surroundings. With my experiences the previous nights, I could not have been more on edge. I nervously rubbed my arms underneath my jacket as I walked to the site of my encounter. I had only a few hours before sunset, long enough to recover my gun and return to my hold, or at least I had hoped.

Returning to the scene of my struggle I looked out across the mire, no sign of the gun my father had left me. The mire held its breath as I searched the area. It seemed finding my gun would be no simple task. I began to dig through the mud, each empty hole feeding the shadow of dread that looked over me. Each new one sparked a light that I might find it, only if I simply dug one more hole in the loose muddy earth beneath me.

False hope can be an intoxicating thing, dear reader. It is but an enemy of common sense that drives forth destruction. It is from that false hope that I did not abandon my search as soon as I should have done. That hope tempted me to stay, crawling through the reeds for any sign of a familiar glint of wood or metal. Perhaps the smell of black gunpowder could alert me to its hiding place.

These sparks and flickers of hope wrapped themselves around my heart, and as the sun set, I pushed the feelings of dread from my mind. This weapon meant more than just the sense of safety and protection it granted. I would not have it claimed by the fens! As the sun dropped below the horizon, I carried on with my search. I seemingly had half an hour of remaining light to find it. Foolishly, I trusted my senses to return me to safety, even after the fall of darkness. As the last bits of light faded from the cold grasp of the marsh, I stood feeling a great despair. I had spent hours looking, yet it would seem I had lost my father's last gift to me. How he would have scolded me for it if he were still here.

As I grieved the loss of my father's gun, I looked

around the pitch-black bog. I cursed my luck and the hope that had guided me here. Looking up at the sky, I saw the twinkling light of stars, like small lanterns alit across the sky. A sense of fear had withheld me from taking a lantern of my own, but how desperately I needed one at that moment.

I am unsure as to how long I wandered under the faint light of the moon. I kept watch for the light of a lantern as I trudged in the direction I thought led home. The fens moved under my feet, shifting like a maze with no end. From the corner of my eye I saw it, the flicker of lantern flame. I turned toward it with surprise, only to find a familiar dark silence echoing back. It was clear my mind had been befuddled with paranoia after my encounter with the creature. From the edges of my vision I would see lantern flames alight, only to be quenched upon my focus. With each light my pace grew faster, fear coursing through me as I went.

Soon I began to question the falseness of these lights. Was it simply tricks of the mind driven by fear and darkness, or was something far more sinister following my trail. I had been wandering the mire for a long time now, surely had it been the day I should have reached my door. Yet across the marsh, only a dark silence answered back. No sounds filled the marshlands, as if it were scared to even breathe. I nearly felt the same. The more quickly I questioned my sanity the quicker I dismissed the thought. Was this light simply hallucinations of the mind? Had it all been? It all felt too real. As I contemplated whether my mind was sound, I saw a flickering light emanating behind me. For a moment I froze, unable to move as its hideous gaze moved across my back. Slowly, I turned towards the source of the light.

A familiar lantern swung forth from a long oak staff. It was him—the very same creature made its way towards me. This time I knew it intended for my demise. I felt the earth beneath my feet. It squished but did not give way under my weight, a stroke of luck. In this solid section of the marsh I could keep pace with its stride. There was no time for panic. Quickly, I used the creature's light to familiarize myself with the terrain. This stretch of solid ground only went another 30 steps before plunging back into the soaking wet bog. I looked back towards the creature, its misshapen body moving through the mire beside me, refusing to touch solid ground—or the moment.

I saw a familiar log half buried in the mud. By the light of this strange being, I suddenly knew the way back. With speed unbefitting of my exhaustion, I jumped far, my legs plunging into the muck before moving in the direction of my hold with great haste. At my fastest pace, I managed to move slightly ahead of the monster. I could not keep this pace long, though I was not far from my shelter in this swamp. Using its light, I waded through the muck with haste. It's light shining from behind me, gilding the path before me with its strange light. Soon I saw the cobbled wall of my home. This light, an affront to all that is holy, had guided me back. As I trapped myself within my hold, I questioned its significance. Scratching at my arms, I began to worry. Was it here for a reason? For what reason would God allow such a wretched thing to exist. Had I done something worthy of such haunting?

These thoughts stewed in my mind as I looked out through the fogged glass window. It stood outside, still. Almost as if it was waiting for me to invite it inside my abode.

"You will receive no such invitation!" I called as I began to barricade the door as I had done the night before. I would have liked to spend the rest of the night watching and waiting in suspense. However, now that I had reached relative safety, I felt my exhaustion begin to return. Before I could finish my barricades, I succumbed to my weariness.

As morning light trickled in, I made a vow. A vow to myself to leave this place, for staying any longer could only be accomplished but the most foolish of men. Was it God telling me to leave this place? If otherwise, why would he allow this creature to haunt me so. As I vowed my leave, I checked myself over, grime clinging to my arms as if it were holding on for dear life. I noticed discolorations across my legs—bruises viscous to the touch, unlike how any normal wound should manifest. Something strange had taken its hold of me. I felt it deep within my soul. If I did not leave now, I may never leave again.

I packed my belongings and readied myself for the long journey across the swamp. It would take a day and a half, however if I kept a fair pace, I would probably shorten the journey a good many hours. I only brought a single bag with me, basic supplies for I had lost my only sentimental artifact to the fens themselves. I could feel the bog revealing with its stolen heirloom. As I started my journey, I bid farewell one last time. First to the hold I had called home for many years, then to my father for it felt as if the bog had taken him as well.

I wandered from morning to evening, not daring to take time for rest. Lest I allow the sun to set and find myself as I was the previous night. The ground became more solid as it rose, my feet sinking less and less into the earth. As I left the fenlands, I vowed I would never return. I would live a simple life away from the swamp, abandoning the lands my family once swore to keep watch over. The creature was free to do as it wished, for I would not die there.

For the time being, I took residency at an inn in a nearby village. Here I decided I would stay until I figured out what was to come next. I had escaped the fenlands themselves, but I had yet to escape the grief and strife that came with it. Memories of my father came to the forefront of my mind. Abandoning the land my family swore to protect weighed heavy on my soul, yet I knew it would be the end of me had I stayed.

Over the next few dawns, I began to notice my body weakening—bog stains and widening brushes refusing to leave my skin. I found myself riddled with nightmares, and cursed by a newfound attraction towards the glow of lantern light, as if I were a moth to a flame.

Dear reader, something within me is changing. I have called for the aid of a priest, yet I am afraid this will be the end of me. I believe myself to have yet a matter of days before my unfortunate demise. So, I write a warning to all who wander near the marshes. Be watchful and take heed, for in the pursuit of knowledge, my fate is contagious.

KNUTS

EMMA BLACKWELL

CONTENT WARNINGS:
Death, cancer, mental illness

I stand at the front door of my childhood home, thinking about how a year ago I was celebrating my 22nd birthday with my parents. The morning brisk December air seeped through the windows. I made food while my mom set up my Christmas tree and my dad sat on the couch playing light holiday tunes on his guitar. But now they are dead.

They died a month later on the U.S. 101 coming home from Lincoln City. They wanted to go to a beach house all the way up on the Oregon Coast to celebrate another year of being together. It was cold and rainy when they were leaving Oregon and close to hitting the California border. A semi-truck took a sharp turn too wide and hit my parents going in the opposite direction.

I'm looking at my reflection in the dirty, smudged glass next to the door. I look terrible; the messy brown hair from my nap on the airplane and my glassy green eyes. I don't think my heart has ever thudded louder in my life. I raise my hands and watch them shake. This is my first time being home since they died. All the time I have spent crying, screaming, and drowning myself in my bed hasn't helped at all. Every day, I just miss them more and more. As the days pass without them my anxiety is becoming more unbearable. My worst nightmare was losing my parents, and here I am. Everyone told me that with time, grieving will become easier and that I will realize they are in a better place, but in my opinion, that's a complete lie. From day one, it has felt like I am going to hear my phone ring and hear their voices on the other side. But dead people can't call.

I hear a car door shut behind me. I turn to see a tall blonde lady walking towards me on the porch.

"Hello, I'm Lacy Scotch, with Primer Real Estates. Are you Rachel or Dave Marshall?" she says, holding out her hand. I can't help but think how annoyingly chipper she sounds for it being in the late afternoon and her day should almost be over.

"I'm their daughter, Lennon," I say, putting my hand out to meet hers.

"Oh, perfect. We have been trying to get in contact with the owners, but the numbers we had on file seemed to be disconnected."

"Yeah, this was my parents' house, but they died a year ago. I inherited the house. Why are you here? Is there something wrong? I was receiving a few calls from the neighbors about someone coming by, if I knew it was a real estate company I would've called."

Rue lived across the street. He was close to my parents. Rue always said I was the kid he and his wife Ellie could never have. For the last two weeks, I've ignored his calls about people coming by. I haven't talked to Rue since my parents died. Seeing him at their funeral and noticing how much older he's getting broke something inside of me. I didn't want to face losing another person in my life.

"Oh no, the house is perfect! We heard that no one was living in the house and I'm here to see if you are interested in selling it. So many people would love a house like this." She pulls out a folder from her bag.

"If you want we can set up a time later this week to get an appraisal on the home and get it up on the market as fast as possible!" She opens the folder and hands it to me.

Inside I see a photo of my parents standing in front of the house. I read their old phone numbers, their email addresses, and I can see their old bank information. I am about to break. My heart's beginning to race, I feel the thuds trying to jump out my body. Can she see my puffed red eyes from the constant crying? Can she tell I'm starving and unable to eat because I am petrified to be home? Can she tell I want her to fucking leave my house already? Can she tell the anxiety is getting to me?

"Alright, you need to leave. I am not interested in selling the house. Please take this folder back with you and throw it at the bottom of the files and never come here again." I say with my voice beginning to break. Panic sets in even more.

"Okay, but in case you change your mind, here is my business card. Before I leave, I need to update the fine information. What's your address and phone number?" She is still in a good mood, which frankly is making me mad. And I can feel the sweat in my palms apart to make its way in between my fingers from keeping them clenched.

"You don't need that from me, this is my home. Please just leave."

"Well I presume you are not living here since I've been here a few times, so I need the information if anyone is interested in buying the house," she says, flashing her happy devilish grin.

"No one is buying this home. Now leave," I respond, turning around sharply and making my way to the front door.

"It's okay, sweetie, take your time. I'll be out here waiting for you and your contact."

This lady is crazy. I told her to leave and she's choosing

to stay. What is wrong with these companies these days and their employees? As I turn the doorknob, the door slowly falls open and I gaze into the remnants of my family. I think I forgot how to blink. My eyes are searing but still wet from the tears.

The door shuts behind me, and I immediately press my back to the door and slide down letting faint sounds escape my mouth from trying to hold my tears back. The panic has now fully set in. I can't breathe and everything feels like it is spinning. I started seeing a therapist after my parents' accident and was diagnosed with generalized anxiety disorder. When I talked to him about Rue's calls, he thought it would be good for me to come back and learn how I can fully process their death as well as see how their passing affects my anxiety.

I throw my bag next to me and I hear the loud metal-like clank explode through the room as it hits the ground. I look down and see the reflective metal leaf barely poking out of my hardly unzipped bag.

I remember my dad telling me about the flowers. He and my mom met in college. My mom was the smart one, and my dad was only there because his parents made him. My mom told him to follow his dreams. That semester, he dropped out of college and went to trade school. He became a welder and how he makes her a new one every year to show his gratitude and his love for her.

The feeling of the cold metal against my hand brings me out of my spiraling thoughts. The only thing that came out of my parents' accident besides the obliterated car and my endless depression was the single flower my dad welded for my mom out of knuts, bolts, and other miscellaneous nails and screws.

I can't hold back the tears anymore, I am fixated on my house and how I feel no child should have to talk into their childhood home without their parents welcoming them. Forcing myself up off the ground, I begin to make my way through our home. Everything has been left the exact way it was when they died. Going through the living room, to the kitchen, to every other room in the downstairs and my body is still trembling. I make my way up the stairs. I see every school photo of myself from kindergarten to college on the wall. My parents were the people who lived off of memories. Constantly taking photos, and telling me never to grow up.

My skin burns as I see the double doors that mark the entrance to my parents' room. I can feel the scratching beneath my skin, and the air around me goes stiff and it's immediately harder to breathe again. I can feel the acid in my stomach begin to flip and pester my organs with pain, anxiety taking over my body.

I let air guide the door open. I take a single step forward, and my feet stop moving beneath me. My eyes pan the room. On the wall to my left is an array of family photos. On the right wall there is a massive window out looking at the front yard. I feel my body hit autopilot and I stand square to the wall, looking at every single flower my father welded for my mother. Each one is dated with their anniversary.

I look down into my hand and see that I am carrying the newest one. The 35th one. I see the lone space that was created probably just a few hours before they left on their weekend getaway. I see the small lip sticking out from the wall, I place the newest welded flower on the lip, taking a step back with my eyes scanning the rows of metal flowers.

I can feel my parents' bed hit the back of my knees. Being home again makes me miss everything about my childhood. It was a simpler time; as a kid I was always wrapped-up in board games, sports, playing outside or anything that kept my young mind occupied. Now I am facing the old dusty walls of the place where my parents had given me everything and I was never able to give them it all back.

I fly down the stairs as I hear a knock coming from the front door. *I swear if this young blond lady with the animated personality is standing on the other side of the door when I open it, I am going to grab one of the stones from the walkway in front of my house and throw it through her car window.*

"Lennon, you got my voicemails. I saw a car in front of the house and noticed the vultures found you before I could," he says, looking over his shoulder, pointing out the young lady.

The man standing in front of me is definitely not Miss Perfect Lacy Scotch. His hunched shoulders, stringy gray beard, and the short black walker with neon yellow tennis balls attached to the feet of his walker, revealing he has aged since I saw him last.

"Rue, I haven't seen you in forever. What are you doing here?" I say dumbfounded, quickly wiping my wet face and putting on the best smile I can.

"Good to see you kid. I was waiting for you to come back, and I sat outside on my porch every day since the first time I called you," he says.

"I wasn't planning on coming back, but you know therapists. He told me I needed to come before things got worse with people coming to my house. I was planning on calling you back. But since seeing you at their funeral, I got scared."

"You know, when my wife Ellie died, the same real estate agency came by my place. It was a young gentleman though who was a lot less put together than the lady you got out there." He lets out a little chuckle, which turns into an elderly wet and thick cough. I step out of the house and guide him to sit next to me on the porch swing.

"I was hoping you would come back here after you

graduated. The neighborhood has been pretty quiet since you grew up and moved to the other side of the country."

"At first, I was just really dedicated to having a good job post-graduation. But then the accident happened, and it's been hard with them not being here." I look down at my shaking hands and hope Rue doesn't notice.

"I don't think I've ever been this angry. I've been working so hard for them, and it feels like they are still here. I just miss them so much. Nothing seems worth it anymore if they aren't here to see it," I say, looking up.

"I've known Rachel and Dave since they bought this house. I promise you they see your accomplishments and struggles. More than anything, they would want you to be happy and live a full life." Rue says.

"Look, you caught me at a bad time. But thank you for sto-" I say before getting cut off.

"C'mon, let me take you to the store. You're going to need food in the house since I assume you're going to be here for a bit." He seems to sense that I need a break from the house.

We walk across the street, Lacy keeping her eyes on us the entire time. It seems like she wants to stop me again and ask, but thankfully for Rue, she left me alone.

"What did you do?" I ask.

"Slipped her a Benjamin and a coupon for a deep tissue massage," he says with a loud laugh.

I can't help but let out a faint chuckle.

Looking into the supermarket on 7th Street is weird. It's like looking back at my childhood. I am standing in front of the automatic doors, staring in disbelief. Nothing about the store has changed either. It's like the world is trying to push me over the edge.

As my eyes guide the room, I can imagine myself running straight to the seasonal section during Halloween, trying to find the mini pumpkin sugar cookies. Then a few months later, trying to convince my parents that our Christmas decorations were old and dated and how we really needed new ones. I can picture myself standing at the checkout lanes begging my mom for a Snickers bar, and the slow short tempered ladies they always had working. I can imagine all the balloons we've picked up here for the endless amount of birthday parties.

"Look lady, are you gonna walk in or stand there?" the woman working register one says to me, waving a hand.

"Right, sorry." I walk into the store and turn my head as the loud, slow screeching of the automatic door fills the room. I look around for Rue, but I don't see him. I walk slowly through the supermarket and the sounds of mothers, fathers, and their kids fill my ears. My head is on a swivel, constantly looking at each family I pass by. Nerves begin to set in. This is my first time being here without them. I feel hot, the minuscule balls of sweat forming at my hairline. I shake my hands, trying to shake off the tension.

"There you are," Rue says, approaching me in one of those scooter carts. I push my hands down onto my side quickly turning around to face Rue.

"Man, you really got old on me if you need one of those," I say, trying to cover the shakiness in my voice.

"Hey, Lennon, I actually wanna talk to you about something." He says.

"Yeah?"

"Four months ago, I was diagnosed with cancer. Lung cancer specifically." Rue says.

What the actual fuck.

My feet freeze beneath me. I am staring at the ground in silence. My breath hitches,, and there is no way to control my body's tremors.

"Look, I know this is really hard for you. You came home to grieve, and here I am telling you I am going to die. But Lennon, you need to know. I needed to tell you because you know how hard it is knowing when my time comes, a random person at the hospital is going to call you and tell you I'm gone. I can't do that to you again."

"Uh, I ca- ca- can't breathe." I stutter out.

Rue brought me back to the house. It took a while to get out of the store. The silence of my home makes me restless. Every old creek from the floorboards, every tick from the clock going in constant, endless circles, and every vibration coming from the cars driving on the rainy road in front of the house. The tears begin dribbling down my cheeks. Rue is sitting next to me, I can tell he's upset.

"How long have you been dealing with these panic attacks?" He says breaking the silence.

"Since they died."

"Lennon, I love you like my own. I don't want to see you hurt any more than you are."

"How am I supposed to go back to Boston knowing the last parental figure in my life is dying?" I say, crying.

"It's not easy, but when you're as old as I am, you learn a lot from it."

"What do you learn that everyone dies and you spend the rest of your life in pain waiting for them?"

"Precisely that. Look, I need help. I don't have anyone left here. Why don't you consider moving back home? You can help me with my appointments, and I can help you live."

Is he crazy? I have a life in Boston. I have a job, an apartment, and a cat. I have a fucking cat named Pickles, and Rue is allergic to cats. But California is home. My therapist would tell me to do this. He would say something along the lines of "Healing is the first step to success and how taking the initiative to heal is the hardest part."

"Fine, but you're not going to like Pickles."

"Pickles?"

"My cat. And you have to promise me that I'm not

going to lose you without being okay."

"I promise Lennon."

5 Months Later

"Hello, everyone. Thank you for coming here today in celebration of Rue Gardner. Everyone, please look at your schedules to see when they are speaking. Rue was a kind soul who lived every day with a smile on his face and in the light of god."

"Hello, everyone. My name is Lennon Marshall. I've never been really religious. I don't remember the last time I stepped inside a church. For it being a second home for so many people, I'm glad I'm here being a part of Rue's community and gathered here with you all today. I grew up in the house across the street from Rue. He was always family to me. He was there to wish me goodbye on every single first day of school, he was there after my first breakup in high school, and he was there when I went off to college. But most importantly, Rue taught me what it's like to live. A year and a half ago I lost my parents in a tragic car accident. I was never able to grieve their deaths, and it caused me to have a lot of issues facing anxiety. Although I lost contact with Rue during the years I spent away. He was there when I needed him the most. Rue taught me the importance of loving yourself. I moved back home after he told me he was diagnosed with cancer. And I am so glad I was there when he rang the bell and kicked cancer's ass. I didn't even realize he made me his emergency contact until I got the call from the hospital that he missed a doctor's appointment, and they told me his cancer had come back and that he was dying. I want everyone to know that Rue was never in pain his last few days. He spent them here in this building after leaving the hospital against the doctor's orders. In the last 5 months, I talked to Rue every day. Rue took the time to help me learn how to grieve. If any of you here are struggling with losing Rue or anyone else in your life. Just remember pain is temporary, and no matter how much you miss them, they are always with you. You may not be able to see them or hear their voice, but love ties you together. Rue taught me this, and let's always remember to love one another, but more importantly ourselves. Thank you, Rue, for living a long and fulfilled life. Thank you for showing me and so many others they can as well. And I can't wait for the day in the future when I get to run home to you and my parents in heaven."

I walk off the podium, hearing the claps and sobs from the people behind me. I sit back down in my chosen spot on the pews, reach into my pocket, and pull out the 35th flower. When Rue was in the hospital, we passed the flower back and forth to each other when we needed a little extra love to get through the day. Right now, I am looking at the slight change we made to the flower. Rue and I painted rusted knuts we found in his garage and glued them together. They sit at the bottom of the stem. We did this so the flower is now able to stand. Rue told me even old and broken things are always able to stand in the end.

Time and Regret

Reigen Komagata

Regret is a heavy burden
on the soul, stones left
unturned and words
not said. All I want
is one more chance
to try again, to talk
to you, to see you
one more time

More time is all
I want, but time doesn't stop
for anyone, haunted
by the sense of time,
no time left to make
new memories, but it is within
the memories that their spirit
will forever reside

as with the sun,
it will break the cold
lonely nights, these haunting
memories drag me back, a reminder
that life is fragile, to cherish
those around us.

Yet I always end up back
to the place I thought I had left
to say thank you,
and I love you
but regret
Is all I am left with

FROM THE RIBCAGE
GRACIE SHOEMAKER

It was a small, pale white jewelry box. Shaped like a heart, the ceramic showed a hand-painted image of roses on the lid. Painted on the inside was a name and year. Augustine, 1980. It was mine.

"Look at this!" a young woman exclaimed, rushing to pick up my jewelry box. She cradled it in her hands, gently lifting the lid and peering inside.

I looked up at her, tilting my head to squint into her eyes. She couldn't see me. She felt very warm though. "There's a name, too! I think it says..."

"Augustine. That's someone's name. That box looks super haunted. We don't need a ghost in our dorm," her companion said, fidgeting with her hands. I stared at her. She glanced up as I did, her eyes passing through me. She shivered. She could feel me, I knew it.

"I'm getting it anyway. I don't care," the first girl said.

"Alright, Evelyn, but it's your ghost," the second retorted, throwing her hands up and walking off.

"You'll love her, Nellie," Evelyn giggled, following her friend. They wandered to the front desk, purchased my box, and ran through the rain to get to their car. I slid silently into the backseat and stared out the windows. It had been so long since I'd been outside and away from all the others. I was excited and a little nervous, too. I didn't know where I was going, but I didn't have much of a choice.

It was much quieter here than it was in the antique store. There was always a constant stream of people, and each of them always walked right past me, ignoring me. After the second or tenth time, it got frustrating. I tried speaking to them, touching them, or following them around the store, but it didn't make a difference.

It was much warmer here, too.

The people that lived here were in and out quite a bit. I came to learn that they were students. All four of them spent all day running in and out of the front door; going to work, classes, or meetings. Their schedules worked out so usually there was someone home, but it still got lonely.

Evelyn kept my jewelry box in her room, but I often left to wander the rest of the apartment. I liked to sit at the windows and watch the clouds roll in, and when it came, the rain. I couldn't leave the apartment though. When I tried to, there was a tug at my chest, like an invisible rope that connected me to my box. That's really all I knew about it. Nobody at the antique store knew either.

On top of the fridge was a statue of a goose. She was dressed up as a witch in preparation for "spooky season." It made her look a little funny. They named her Lucifer, or Lucy for short.

Across from the kitchen was the living room, separated by a breakfast bar. In the corner of the living room was a lamp with a plastic unicorn skull resting on top. His name was Fredrick. When I got too lonely, or it got too quiet, I spoke with Lucy and Fredrick. They didn't respond, but their painted eyes did. They were much better company than the haunted dolls my box used to be next to. The dolls were snotty brats who only spent their time gossiping about people who walked by.

One night, Evelyn and Nellie decided to watch a scary movie. They hung a sheet against the wall, and Nellie got a box that made really big pictures on the wall. They made snacks, got blankets, and curled up on the couch beside each other.

I stuck around for the movie. It was scary, but I didn't like when they jumped at the picture or screamed. They would always look at each other and laugh, so I left it alone.

When it ended, both of them jumped at any creak or movement. Several times, Nellie got up to look out the door's peephole into the hallway.

"Want to watch another one?" Nellie asked Evelyn, who nodded with a grin.

Nellie hunted for another movie, and Evelyn searched for some more snacks. Nellie found what she was looking for, and another image from the box appeared on the wall. Evelyn settled in next to her, and they began to watch the next movie. Every couple of minutes, they would scream or have to get up and make sure the door was locked.

After an hour of this, I had enough. I hated it, I hated how they were scared. This wasn't fun. I went up to the sheet and ripped it right off the wall. Both of them screamed and leaped from the couch.

"I'm sorry, Augustine! We'll be done! We'll go to bed!" Nellie laughed, fear trickling into her voice. No, don't be afraid. I wasn't trying to scare you, I wanted to tell them.

"How do you know it's Augustine?" Evelyn said, gathering the dishes that used to hold the snacks.

"I don't, it's just a feeling. Growing up, I had ghosts in my house, and they did stuff like this. That sheet was duct taped to the wall. It couldn't have just fallen. Besides, it's almost 1 in the morning. We should probably get to bed anyway."

"You think she was telling us to go to bed?"

"Why not? If I was a ghost and people were being loud, I wouldn't like it very much."

I didn't like it, but not because you were loud. I didn't

like seeing you scared.

Nellie was gone a lot. Every Friday, she rushed into the apartment, throwing things into a bag, grabbing her car keys, and rushing out again. Then she didn't come back for a couple of days.

I don't know where she goes, but I don't like it very much. Why couldn't she stay where I could see her? Where I know what's going on and I could keep her safe?

I went to her room. The door was locked. She locked it every time she left for a few days.

With a quick *pop* of my hand inside the lock, the door swung open. I stepped into the room, grinning. What's in here that I can use to make her come back? I searched her room for something, anything that could work. *There!*

On the wall is a picture. It's got bright blue and pink colors, with some people I've never seen before. It's in a black frame, too, and I remember Nellie getting excited when it came in the mail.

I reached up the wall and pulled it loose.

With a loud *bang!* it fell off the hooks that were holding it up. It crashed to the ground, sliding between the wall and Nellie's bed. I grinned. *That was fun!* It slid so fast and made such a fun noise!

When Nellie got back, she was not happy. When she stepped in front of her door, she froze, and all the color drained from her face.

"Did you guys open my door?" she asked the others, who were in the hall, celebrating her return.

"No. Did you not lock it? We don't have keys either," Evelyn said, shrugging.

"I did lock it! I double-checked!" Nellie said, tears coming to her eyes. She turned to face Evelyn, her lip trembling. "I'm really freaked out now."

Maybe you won't leave next time.

She stepped into her room and immediately gasped. She dropped her stuff to the floor, and Evelyn stepped into the room behind her.

"What is it?"

"My poster fell off the wall, and there is absolutely no way that could have happened. There are so many hooks that are holding that poster up." Nellie stopped and stared at the now-empty wall for a moment. "Augustine. I bet she did it."

I watched from just outside the door. *I did it. I knocked it off the wall, and you came back.*

"Why would she do that?" Evelyn asked, tilting her head a little.

"I don't know. But how else can you explain my door being unlocked?"

Evelyn shrugged and walked back to the kitchen.

Nellie turned to the hallway where I was standing. She looked into my eyes for a moment, but her gaze settled on my nose. I know she couldn't see me, but it was still unsettling how close she got.

"Leave my stuff alone, Augustine. I'm happy to be your friend, but not if you're breaking my things," Nellie said, tears still in her eyes.

I'm sorry. I didn't do it to scare you, I just wanted you to stay here with me.

Nellie and I have made up since that day. Whenever I have the energy to, I knock on the walls around the apartment just to let everyone know that I'm still here. Each time I do, Nellie responds with a knock of her own.

There was a morning when it was just her and I. Everyone else had already left for the weekend, each doing their own thing. Nellie reeked of loneliness and was lost in her own world. She stumbled into the kitchen, rubbing sleep from her eyes. As she passed the front door, I knocked as loud as I could.

She paused, the sleep gone. She stared at the door, right at my hand. "Hi Augustine," she said, and went back to finding something for breakfast.

Hi, I wanted to say back. *You're not alone,* I wanted to say. *I'm right here for you.*

Later that same day, Nellie was still very lonely. I could tell. It radiated off of her like light from Fredrick's lamp.

She was on the couch, with her back to the door. I hated seeing any of them like this. I knew there were friends in the building; they just needed an invitation.

With an incredible amount of energy, I unlocked the door and swung it open. It was very heavy, but it kept itself mostly open. I stepped back, admiring my handiwork.

It took Nellie a while to notice. When she did, she jumped off the couch and slammed the door shut, locking it quickly. She then paced the apartment, checking each of the rooms. Seemingly satisfied, she flopped back onto the couch, wrapping up in a blanket.

She was still lonely, though. I could tell.

So I opened the door again. It took her longer to notice this time. When she did, she was not happy.

"Augustine," Nellie called out softly, a hint of frustration in her voice. She got up and shut the door again, making sure the lock clicked into place. "You can't open the door, okay? I'm fine. Just a little lonely is all. But the door needs to stay shut."

Oh. Okay.

Spent, I went back to Evelyn's room. My jewelry box was on her desk. I sank into it, and waited for the others to come home.

It was loud. I wandered down the hallway towards the kitchen, where the noise was coming from. Everyone was there, including some friends who had been coming around more.

"That's not what we're saying," Nellie said, frustration clear in her voice and body. She was standing in front of the sink, scrubbing a pan from earlier in the day.

"Then what are you saying?" Evelyn responded. She was at the kitchen counter, a pad of paper and a pen in front of her.

"I can't figure out how to phrase it right," Nellie said, soap from the sponge flying all over the counter. That happened pretty often.

They continued going back and forth, growing louder and louder. I slapped my hands over my ears, but I could still hear them arguing.

You aren't supposed to fight! I yelled, but I was left ignored. I could feel the air grow thicker around me, alight with electricity and tension. Their voices became deafening.

I had enough. I walked to the front door and knocked twice, as loud as I could. Everyone turned to look at the door, and me. "Hi, Augustine," everyone said at once. They all turned back to each other and broke down laughing. The tension immediately disappeared.

That's much better.

Something was going on. There were boxes all over the apartment, and almost all of them were half full. The "vibes," as they were called, were off. Everyone was in a slump, and tears were shed almost every night.

"What are we going to do with this?" Nellie asked Evelyn, holding up a banner that had been hung on the wall.

"I'll take it with me. I have a spot in my room at home it'll fit in."

"What about this?" she asked, holding up my box.

"I... I don't know. I don't have anywhere to put Augustine," Evelyn replied, ducking her head. "And I don't think she'll get along with your ghosts at home."

"She won't. She's too nice. Could we donate her box? Then she'll stay on campus?"

"We could. I think the donation center is open, but it closes soon. If we go now, we could make it," Evelyn said, already reaching for her shoes. Nellie scrambled after her, picking up my box. She cradled it, and I followed her out the front door.

After rushing across several parking lots and dragging me with them, Evelyn and Nellie stopped in front of a set of tables.

"Are you guys still open?" Evelyn asked, out of breath.

"We are. What can I help you with?" the table attendant asked, reaching for a clipboard.

"We want to donate this. It's important that it stays on campus," Nellie panted, also out of breath from running. She held out my box to the attendant, who took it with a strange look.

"Thank you," they both said at the same time.

"Bye, Augustine," Nellie said quietly.

"Bye, Augustine," Evelyn whispered, waving a little at my boc.

What? What do you mean, bye? You're leaving?

With that, they both turned and walked away. Together, they glanced at me one more time. Nellie looked straight into my eyes and smiled. She knew.

After I was left at the table, I sank into my box and stayed there for a long time. I could feel that I had been moved a couple of times, but each time I opened my eyes, it was dark. This time was different. My box was on the table again, and it was still warm. I felt a chill in the air, though. It would get colder soon.

"Look at this box!" a woman called out. She was young, and her eyes were very excited. There was another young woman behind her who looked nervous.

"I don't know. It's cute, but it gives haunted vibes," her friend said quietly.

"Perfect! A new friend for our brand new dorm!"

"But what if it's a mean ghost?"

I'm not mean. Only a little lonely.

"She feels nice," the first one said. "We'll take her!"

FOR A MOMENT
TERYN TOMINAGA

"How absurd! A machine that lets people converse from across the country?" Clara Bolt's twittering voice rang out, cutting through the stillness of the dying land. With the coming of winter, the Oak trees encompassing the cemetery boasted bright red leaves that gleamed in the moonlight.

"Across the world, even." Their newest addition—by just over a century or so—had been buried just over a week ago. Steven Korch, dead by his own means of over-intoxication. The inhabitants of the cemetery flocked to his burial the night he arose, and Steven was only too eager to entertain their wonders about the present world.

"Impossible!" Clara exclaimed.

"It's true." Ernie Collar piped up. Until then, he'd been the youngest departed soul. "Clara, I told you about this when I first arrived, don't you remember?"

"No, I don't."

"A weird-looking thing, the handset being-"

"Oh no it's different now," Steven interrupted. "Now it's about this wide, and this flat, and you hold it to your ear and speak into it." Steven held up his hands to display the dimensions of this phone.

Dr. Johnathan Rothan, dubbed Johnny Rotten by his fellow deceased, stood off to the side, bordering the congregation. He listened to Steven's words growing more bored by the minute. It wasn't that what the youth spoke of was uninteresting. In fact, it was quite fascinating. But on the other hand, Johnny still had no idea what the present was like outside of its technological advancements.

"And you can even do this thing called FaceTime, where you press a green button on the screen and you can see the person." Steven, grinned looking around, clearly loving the bafflement of the older—to put it generously—crowd. However, their blank stares simply could not convey the disbelief the youth wanted, for he frowned and scratched his head, flakes of gray skin and crusted mud falling out.

Johnny sighed. The boy would just have to learn how to read the subtle tells of the restricted canvas, that was the human skeleton, in time. Soon enough, the boy's own muscles, sinews, and other soft tissue would dissolve or get consumed by the critters of the earth, and he too would be stuck with the clench or parting of the jaw and the tilts and swivels of the head.

"What about automobiles?" Ernie Collar asked, coming around to perch on Steven's tombstone. Ernie had died in a house fire during the turn of the twentieth century when the assembly line had just been popularized. Tufts of crinkled brown hair could be seen on half of his skull, while the other half exhibited vast streaks of charred bone, blackened and brittle.

"Man, I had this one Chevy that could push two hundred easy. Miles per hour." Steven added in response to their silence.

Jeffry Holdstetter chuckled, slapping his hands on his kneecaps before rising from where he sat atop Steven's burial mound. "You mistake us for fools, Steven."

"I'm telling the truth!"

Johnny thought he was lying.

"Dear, it doesn't do any good to boast about such ludicrous things. Over 200 miles an hour, I mean really,"

Clara cooed.

Johnny hoped he was telling the truth.

"And airplanes!" Steven said desperately, leaning towards old man Guill.

"Air planes?"

"I bet you guys traveled on a boat or something, right, to get across oceans. But nowadays, we fly!"

Johnny laughed, shaking his head. "I don't know whether or not to believe you. The things you speak of are laughable at best. But who could come up with such crazy ideas and speak of them so confidently, they have to be true."

Steven turned to him, grinning widely now. A tear appeared on his graying cheek, near the corner of his mouth, revealing bands of decaying muscle, and Johnny watched with fascination as a couple of maggots, who were buried deep within, toppled out.

"They are! I am! Telling the truth-"

"When were these airplanes of yours built?" Lady Algeraldi, the oldest—in life and in death—of their congregation, asked. She'd already been plotted in the earth when the cemetery had been established in 1847, with only a name engraved into her headstone—more of a small boulder than an actual monument. Able to hold a compelling conversation, she was all but captivating in her wisdom. It was a shame she never came out as much anymore. Perhaps, like Johnny, she grew easily tired of the dead around them.

"Um, I'm not sure. The early nineties?"

"Man conquers the ability to soar above the clouds as birds would, and you cannot remember when such a feat was brought about?"

"Well, it's such a commonplace thing now, so I guess it's not super important to learn about. Learning about Apollo 11, though, when man reached the moon was much more–"

A collective of gasps, laughs, and sighs bounced off the granite monuments, before disappearing into the forest beyond.

"Oh Steven, I had almost begun believing in you," Clara tsked.

Steven smiled and shook his head. "I'll get you guys to come around. You'll see."

"To reach the moon," Old Man Guill marveled, turning his face up.

In turn, they all tilted their craniums up to look at the moon. It beamed down at them, defining the cracks, crumbles of their dwindling remains. Johnny's initial fondness of the moon had disappeared over the years. Their insignificance, despite the collective of many lifetimes, was never more palpable when facing something so timeless. Insignificant and yet he wondered if the moon was ever lonely in the vast sky of dying stars. He hoped not.

"And the people, Steven?" He asked.

The boy's eyes, liquifying slowly in their sockets, turned to look at him.

"How are people in the present?"

"I don't know. Pretty fucked up I guess."

Clara gasped.

"How so?"

Steven shrugged, "Comparably to your time?"

"Not necessarily." Johnny shrugged.

"I mean, I guess times are better. Women have suffrage."

"Surely not!" Clara exclaimed.

"And same-sex marriage is cool."

"Excuse me?" That was old man Guill.

"And I assume education is a lot more widespread now."

Johnny nodded, "So would the term 'better' be

appropriate in difference to the present being 'fucked up?'"

"Ah- well, I wouldn't be so sure about that."

Johnny waited, as did the other relics, each from their respective past. Steven shifted. His suit, a stark black tweed, already had small holes in it, from which mice and rats had taken a few bites. Green cemeteries, while better for the environment, had the tendency to leave their occupants shortcoming in the fashion department.

"Well," Steven finally spoke. "It's a bit sad but sure, the education is here, but so are the guys who randomly march into the schools deciding to put a couple of bullets through the heads of about twenty children or so. Women can vote, but I know there are equality battles still being fought. Gay marriage comes with a side of prejudice and religious hate. And it's not as if the expulsion of racial segregation and schools of thought got rid of racism itself. Also, the world is burning."

"Ah," Johnny mused. "Enlightenment revealing the despair of humanity."

"Sure, you could... put it that way."

It was unsurprising. And, Jonny thought lamely, depressing- history really did repeat itself. And he, in his deteriorating state, could do nothing but listen and watch as the world turned on itself, a cycle of spins, revolutions, and eras.

On that cynical thought, a whisper of voices reached the ears of the dead. A sigh of murmured words and a shuffle of feet; people- a couple, Johnny reckoned- were coming.

"Quick everyone," he urged.

Old man Guill, who'd been born with a defect in which his right tibia formed much shorter than the left, hobbled quickly away, a frightening sight when he first arose out of the grave back in 1894.

"What was that?" Steven asked, uncertainly coming to

stand over his own burial site as the remaining skeletons scattered.

If he had eyes, Johnny would have rolled them. He lowered himself into the ground- his own sepulture right next to Steven's- soil bubbling as if the earth was one big pot of muddy soup. "It's not exactly a pretty sight for the living to walk into if you think about it."

Steven, following suit, asked, "How can we hear them approach?"

Johnny shook his head, the dirt up to his shoulders now. "We just can, now shut it until you're under."

"What?"

But he was already gone, his body slowly sinking through the soft earth, rotten and squirming with life alike until he hit the initial spot he'd been buried many years ago. Johnny had his room- as he learned he liked to call it- memorized from the five foot eleven by 17 inches dimensions to the twelfth pebble down from his skull that dug into his vertebra, the sharpest of the two hundred and thirty-four.

Counting, he'd found at first, was a way in which he greatly enjoyed passing the time. It had been a great achievement when he'd determined that two thousand five hundred and eighty-seven blades of grass lay in the section of earth between his headstone and Lady Algeraldi's, his leftside neighbor. And just behind his headstone, exactly two dandelion flowers. He treasured them for they grew nowhere else in the graveyard. But of course, he eventually felt obligation rather than gratification so he'd taken to naming the critters. He'd named Angela, the rat who nibbled at the fungi surrounding the cemetery, to Rocky Fiddleston, the mouse who'd burrowed his way to make a cavity by his sacrum.

When he'd grown tired of that, he memorized the names of all the individuals of the graveyard and the dates they'd lived. Many weren't even physically there, cremated, but with a family who sought a place they could visit, yet no longer did.

On and on, he'd filled his years with mindless, meaningless time-consuming tasks, willing away the enclosing suffocation that hardly anything could pierce. He knew only too well the nicks and divots of his room, knew every single root that reached for them from the surrounding oak, knew the constellations by heart after decades of staring at the sky for nights on end. How did the others look at the same sky and not envy the stars, burning up with an unequivocal end? And even now, with the new tales of the present by Steven- he found- did little to ease the stifling air, instead casting the world into a further dismal state. If of course what the boy said was true, and the world was burning as well, he implored it to fizzle up tomorrow. And if it did not, he craved just a moment, for the lines of life and death to not be so blurred.

If he had a heart, it would be hammering against his ribcage, pounding in his ears. But he didn't even have that. He had no physical reaction to the state in which his mind presided, if he did, it might have made it the tiniest bit more bearable. Swamped every day in recurring sentiments, he could do nothing but think- and wish in vain that he could not. He would will them away at times with a roaring that replaced the thoughts about the absence of life in all his death.

So loud he couldn't make out his need for more; a need for an ending, a need for a heart that could race to its content. A need for a purpose. So loud he missed what Steven was saying.

"What?" he mumbled, the soil melting against his moving jaw, before solidifying again.

"I said, it's my godparents!" Steven's voice came to him, clear despite the layers of soil between them.

The new voices reached his ears shortly.

"Keep it short, this place reeks. Probably the boy."

"Lucious!"

But the boots of the man had stalked away, moving laterally along the row Johnny and Steven were in.

There was a heavy sigh. "I'm sorry about him, Steven. He's old, like me, and doesn't have the same appreciation for family anymore. I know you didn't see us much in the past several years. Lucious' back isn't as it was, and my body isn't fit for traveling anymore. I'm only sorry we couldn't see you before... You remember Tommy don't you? He's aged, just like us, turned ten this year. The vet says a house cat doesn't usually live past fifteen. But I think he missed you too. He circles your picture, you know the one that you took after visiting us after your high school graduation? Still causes a ruckus around the house, seems you had an influence on him," she chuckled.

"She's a bit sentimental," Steven's voice reached Johnny again. His tone indicated what he thought of all the sentiment. Johnny ignored him, listening to the woman.

"He's a joy to have, And you were too." There was a pause and, thoughtlessly, Johnny's skeleton rose, sifting through the soil closer to the surface; it had been a while since the living had visited the cemetery. "Life's been a bit hard since we fell out of touch with everyone. But I miss you. I miss you helping me water my garden. Lucious didn't like the purple of the irises, so we tossed them. I was going to get daffodils but..."

Johnny didn't have to know what she was going to say to make up his own conclusions.

"My eyesight and hearing are about shot as well, and no movie, radio station, or book can ever entertain me anymore."

Look at the stars, Johnny thought.

"To be honest Steven, I'm glad you won't have to suffer

the monotony of old age. It's almost hell. I'm sure you're in heaven, you were- you are- such a precious boy."

"Sorry to make you listen to this," Steven's voice reached him again. Johnny, irritated at the interruptions, contemplated telling him to eat dirt.

"I'm glad you lived. Though I supposed it was almost too much at the end. I'm glad you didn't just exist. It's a more exhausting ordeal than you'd ever have imagined."

He's about to do more than just imagine it, Johnny thought.

"I'm doing well though, despite it all. Kataline stops by sometimes, got married to Henry Dorothy—the surgeon— last year. She brings daffodils when I ask, and garlic bread without request. The tall grass is filled with crickets this time of year, and they sing a beautiful song right outside my window at night. If it was Lucious' way, he'd have them all exterminated. And the school band just started going about their rounds, fundraising. I look forward to them the most because, well," she laughed. "I can hear them."

Her laugh was light and was carried away by the mild wind, but it'd been a chime, like the one that Johnny used to have hanging on his front porch- sweet and symphonic.

Footsteps sounded nearby, returning. "Let's go- stop messing with those god-forsaken flowers."

Johnny cursed Lucious, willing the woman to stay, to keep talking about the mundane, as beautifully as he now remembered. But two pairs of footsteps left Steven's grave and eventually retreated into the surrounding oak. Johnny surfaced quickly, without sparing a moment to call out the others, looking in the direction in which the living had withdrawn. He saw a brief glimpse of flowing silver hair that winked back at him. Then, no one. He sighed, dusting off the rest of the soil, and slumped on his tombstone. A rock, unearthed by his movements or by the shoes of the couple, lay by Steven's burial.

Without pausing to think he'd plucked it up and flung it into the forest after Lucious and the woman. He'd just bent down to pick up another when he heard a cry. A woman's cry. He froze, staring at the ground, bones curled around the other rock.

Maybe, there was another woman, unforeseen- conveniently waiting in the forest. But Steven's head popped up, hair askew, dirt falling from his mouth as he spoke. "Wasn't that Milacent?"

"Milacent?" Johnny repeated.

"My godmother. The one who was just here."

"Ah. I couldn't say."

Steven looked at his hand, "What's with the rock?"

"I was wondering," Johnny said slowly., "If your patellar tendon still worked."

"My what?"

"Knee jerk reflex."

"Oh. Well. I don't know. And, uh, I don't think testing is necessary."

"Very well," Johnny said quickly and slid immediately, and as naturally as he could, back into his burial. He ignored the inquisitive comments made by Clara, and the continued futuristic prattling of Steven's, for the rest of the night.

It was exactly one week later. The earth rumbled, a soft sermon of words. No weeping, but many hushed conversations. It was much quicker than Steven's ceremony. There'd been a sobbing mother and many pairs of feet previously. But this time there were exactly nine pairs of feet coming, and then leaving.

Johnny, like many of the deceased in the area, had awakened during the service. But he, unlike the others, prayed- truly for the first time in his existence- that the outcome was not what he feared.

It was with horror and- ashamedly- excitement that he saw a woman with a head full of gleaming silver hair arise from the burial mound that night. Milicent Bildrow 1934–2012. She looked around, apparently in wonder, and Johnny saw her eyes gleam.

"Wow," she said, breath shaking. "The world's so clear."

"Of course silly," Clara tittered.

Milicent, unlike her godson- who had not surfaced despite the chiding of the others- didn't seem to be perturbed at the talking skeleton she met eyes to hollows with; Clara wilted a little in disappointment. However, she didn't even seem to notice her godson next to her, for in the moment her eyes caught on something behind all of them. She walked around them, as if being trapped in a carcass was natural for her, to Johnny's grave. He watched her intently as she moved around the tombstone and came to kneel in front of the flowers.

"Dandelions," she smiled. "They would have looked so beautiful next to irises." She stepped back so that they could bask underneath the radiance of the moon. "But they're beautiful still."

Johnny found his voice then, "Milicent. You're dead."

He cursed inwardly; he probably could have phrased it with a tad more grace. But she only laughed and, above ground, it was even more beautiful; kinder.

"I know that. But, I've woken up to friendly faces, my godson by my side- please forgive him he always tends to oversleep- and dandelions nearby."

Her words, despite being more descriptive rather than saccharine, eased the qualms of his mind.

"Although I have the funniest story about how I passed. See I was here a week ago..."

Johnny cringed, immediately focusing on a different aspect of her person. Like how her arms moved dramatically when storytelling, her eyes danced with light, and the slight nuances in her voice that weren't overbearing as Clara's but instead, sought to engage him in every word, lilting voice blending harmoniously with the world around her. It was then he decided to hope. Hope, maybe not for a lifetime, but for a moment in which the lines of death and life, instead for their distinction, but the seamless blend in which they both may spin together, revolve, and bring about a new era.

SCAR TISSUE

CAROLINE HILL

CONTENT WARNINGS:

Abuse, blood, body horror

The sun creates the seasons, but here, they don't follow the typical pattern. One day, it could be summer, the next, winter, and the duration is never known. The seasons don't come in order, and they could change in an instant. Sometimes, it seems like summer may never end, and other times, the sun hides away. There is no balance. The sun holds the power to manipulate each day.

Fall and winter are safest. The sun does not often make an appearance. It rests, rising and setting closer together. Rainy days soothe my skin, gently washing the pain away. The cold may raise bumps, but they are temporary. I much prefer the cold.

Spring is sometimes pleasant; clouds provide a shield that buffers the rays. The light is more tolerable, leaving mere freckles on my skin. Sometimes, the sun creates beautiful moments, moments of brief joy or laughter, which makes me despise it even more. On days when the rain lets up, the sun sneaks in. It creates rainbows, bright colors painting the sky. I know better than to follow their paths. If I allow myself to chase them, I will only find betrayal and disappointment. There is no pot of gold at the end of the rainbow. I've chased it before, only to find the illusion of hope. And when I got close, the sun emerged from the clouds to damage me once again.

The sun is ill-tempered, a raging ball of fire that disperses its feverous heat. It is summer days that hurt the most. The burns penetrate so deep they leave scars wherever they touch. Some reach so deep that my bones see the sun. Everything withers dry in its harsh rays. A small spark can ignite a roaring blaze. Once it has burnt out, the sun drifts away to rest. Even the trees need a break. They shed their shriveled leaves and go dormant. I hide under more layers. My skin needs time to heal.

This summer has been ceaseless. I do my best to shelter myself from the harsh beams. Sunglasses can't protect my eyes; the light is so harsh it drowns out all the colors. I lock myself away, but not even closed curtains can shield me. I wear as many layers as I can, trying to protect myself, but the sweltering heat that radiates from my burns is unbearable. Even the softest clothes feel abrasive, like sandpaper rubbing my skin raw.

While the sun rests, I tend to my wounds. I look in the mirror, and all I see are scars. Some have healed, leaving extensive trails of twisted tissue in their place. My wounds create a map on my skin, charting every memory as a tangible landmark. Others are still raw, open wounds that fester. The newest addition to my collection still weeps, leaving a deep red path training slowly down my chest. I try my best to clean it up. As I drag the damp cloth across my skin, it stings. This wound needs more protection than others. I dress it with bandages, hoping they will be able to shield it long enough for the river to run dry.

Each morning, the sun rises again, like a threat, daring me to stay put. I try my best to make it through my day, but every reflection is a reminder that I am marred by my scars. Time has not yet taken away their pain.

The torture becomes unbearable, and I can't take any more. "Can you not see that you are killing me? All you do is hurt me! I hate myself because of you, I hate you!" The words pour out of me like a broken dam, though words are not the only things that escape me. Tears begin to roll down my face, sizzling as they trail down my cheeks. Each droplet boils and then evaporates, leaving a trail of blisters down to my jawline. "Leave me alone!" My voice trembled through my sobs.

The seasons shift in an instant. The light from the sun disappears like a flipped switch. Rain begins to pour down, and sharp gusts of wind send shivers through my body. Winter had begun. Cold and dark, but this time, I can't find comfort in its coverage. Even though the sun had caused pain, it pains me to hurt it back.

I can't even feel the blanket that I wrap around myself—the scars and calluses have taken away my ability to feel gentle embraces. In the sun's absence, I don't feel much of anything. I have grown numb.

Through the darkness, I see a glowing light. It illuminates its surroundings differently—it does not drown out the objects around it. I make my way towards it. As I approach the point where the shadow meets the light, I pause. I extend one finger into the light. It does not burn. I step fully into it, treading slowly towards the source. The closer I get, the warmer the air becomes, but it is a different warmth. I sit down in front of the source and examine it. It is contained—small flames in a fireplace surrounded by warm bricks. I close my eyes as the gentle warmth permeates through me. I feel a sense of comfort like never before. When I open my eyes, the comfort diminishes. In the light, though, it is kind and gentle. I see only my scars.

In our galaxy, there are billions of stars, but only one of them has the ability to touch us. The one that reaches us is the one we call our sun. Every person has their own sun. The sun is what provides for us. For many, the sun provides happiness, warmth, growth, and essential nutrients. The sun can either give us a bronzed tan or a blistering burn. Either way, its effects are permanent. Even in its absence, I am weary of new light. I do not give my trust easily. I much prefer solitude to the potential of more scar tissue.

HAPPY HUNTING

ZAK KLEMP

CONTENT WARNINGS:
Death, self-harm, murder, graphic depictions of violence, severe gore, blood

Dear Detective Leo,

Life is a rollercoaster. A series of twists and turns, ups and downs. I was brought into a world of love. Two parents that loved me and cared for me. My father would wheel me around the neighborhood in my red wagon. He would tell me stories from his time in the military. He never saw active duty, but I couldn't care less. I was just happy to hear him talk about carrying another sandbag from one side of the base to the other. As a child, my favorite story was when my father was tasked with digging holes that the soldiers used to relieve themselves. My father had a way of telling stories that made you feel as if you had been experiencing them alongside him for the first time.

My mother, on the other hand, was my rock. She was the part of the rollercoaster that slowed everything and calmed you down. The part of the ride that made you feel like you weren't about to be flung out of your seat and into the nearby parking lot. I always knew I could go to her if anything were wrong or if I was ever sad or down. I always loved how she took the time to listen to me, even when she didn't have a clue about what I was saying. She would always nod her head along and ask questions as I spewed random facts about obscure movies no one had ever heard of before.

My family was everything you could have ever wanted. We had money, a big house, and, most importantly, we had each other. But with all rollercoasters, that first lift always leads to a big drop. My parents got divorced when I was young. Old enough to understand that sometimes people grow apart from one another, but still not old enough to understand how my happy family could suddenly be so disconnected. I still loved my parents, but nothing was ever the same as it once was. Over the years, I got used to splitting my time between the two adults I held so close. Despite feeling comfortable being between two homes, I still felt distant, never feeling as if I belonged to one family or the other.

One day, in junior high, I was called to the office. When I got there, I saw my mother standing in front of the secretary's desk. She seemed to be having a conversation with the secretary, but when I arrived, everything went silent. The secretary lowered her head to avoid my puzzled gaze. My mother turned around and gestured to the car parked outside.

We sat in the front seats as my mother drove aimlessly around the neighborhood. Minutes passed without a noise being made other than the tires rubbing against the asphalt road.

"Where are we going, Mom?" I asked, still not knowing why I had been taken out of school.

"Your-" she paused. She looked as if she was about to cry, not out of sadness or joy but out of confusion.

After what felt like forever, she broke the silence again. "Your father... Your father passed away."

Just like that, my heart dropped just like a rollercoaster does after it reaches the second hill. Life is a roller coaster, a series of twists and turns, ups and downs.

Life after my father's death was quiet. My life had been altered forever, I had been changed forever. I became quiet and reclusive, keeping to myself, never opening up. When I wasn't at school, I spent my time cooped up in my bedroom. My mother became worried about me and how I had very little life outside of my bedroom. As a last-ditch effort to get me to interact with the world again, she sent me to a boarding school about forty minutes away. At first, I resented her for doing this to me, but over time, my mind started to heal. I was forced to interact with people my age again. Over the first few months at that school, I had built a tight-knit group of friends with shared interests in all things science fiction and popular culture. We would spend hours hanging out, talking about the newest movie that had come out that weekend or about the concert we planned on going to the next weekend. We even started a radio station at the school just as an excuse to listen to music together. Freshman year and summer flew by in no time.

It was now sophomore year. I was excited for a new year, excited to hang out with my friends and to make new and dumb memories that only me and my friends would find interesting. Me and my roommate, Cal, sat down in our first-period class together, joking around as we tended to do, and that's when I saw her.

Like a cheesy commercial, everything seemed to slow down, that is, everything except for my heart. Her long, wavy brown hair reflected as the sun peeked through the window. Her face glowed with confidence and beauty. It is cliche to say, but I knew when I saw her that she was the one. She sat a row in front of Cal and me, next to a girl named Barb. After a couple of weeks of daydreaming of her, every waking moment, Cal and my other friends convinced me to talk to her. So, one day before class, I introduced myself alongside Cal. After a brief and awkward conversation, courtesy of myself, she revealed to me her name, Elena. From that moment on, we became a group of friends.

Every moment with her was amazing. It didn't matter if we were talking about her favorite boy band, New Kids on The Block, or if we were hanging out at the beach with our friends. I could have been sitting in a dumpster for all I cared, as long as I was with her and my friends. As the year drove on, we grew closer and closer until I finally asked her out on a date, and without hesitation, she agreed. Ever since that moment, we stayed by each other's side. Whenever we had the chance to be together, we took it. And when she went to her hometown in California over the summers, we would call each other for hours upon hours. Some nights, we would even fall asleep together on the phone. Life is a roller coaster, and I never wanted off of the ride. That was until that ride once again took another drop.

A few years went by, and I was in college. Life was great. I had some great professors, still had my friends, and I finally got a job at a local restaurant. One day, that joy for life took a wild turn. It was a normal day, no rain, and a warm sun shining. The only thing slightly different was a large looming black cloud in the distance. No one paid a mind to it, however. It was the Pacific Northwest; dark clouds were normal this time of year. Elena and I were still together. We had recently moved into a house with Barb and Cal. Our college classes had been canceled for the week because our professors were leading a mountain climbing exhibition. The teachers had done it every year in May, but this time, the professors decided to leave a week earlier than normal. Twenty people total left that morning, many of whom I had become friends with. As the day went on, myself, Elena, Barb, and Cal hung out in our living room, flipping through random channels on the TV, trying to find something to watch. Around midday, the TV was interrupted, a large red "Breaking News" flashed across the screen. The scene cut to the local news anchors.

"Hello everyone, we apologize for interrupting, but we have gotten breaking news that a deadly storm has swept over nearby Mt. Hood." the news anchor reported. "We have little information at this time, but we have been informed that a group of college students climbed the mountain earlier today. Nearby lodges at this time haven't heard from this group and it is unsure of the group's location at this time. We can only hope and pray that those students are safe."

Everyone went quiet, and for the next three days, everyone in the area was glued to the TV. No one dared to peel their eyes from the screen. Day by day, students were found covered in snow and ice. Some were frozen to death, others chattering, alive but unable to use their limbs or respond to questioning. Most hauntingly was one girl who had been saved by another student. She had been freezing and another student noticed, so in an attempt to help her, he grabbed her, held onto her and wrapped himself around her, desperately trying to give her his remaining body heat. When she was found on the third day, she was alive, barely breathing, but alive no less. As for the boy, though, he had been frozen to death for the past two days. He was frozen in such a way that denied the girl any way of wiggling out of his death grip. Luckily for her, though, it was that boy that kept her alive.

Nine dead. Nine people died. Nine friends... dead. Our college set us all up with counseling. The school tried its best, but after one partial session, I lost it. I was reminded of the feelings I had when my mom picked me up from junior high. I was reminded of when my parents split from each other. I was reminded of the pain. In a moment of pure, overwhelming emotions, I launched my fist into a nearby locker. The entire hallway froze. I screamed out in agony, not for my shattered hand, but for the pain that my life was in. I picked myself up and ran out the building.

-The Hunter

Dear Detective Leo,

I hid from everyone for weeks, living under houses and between alleyways. Eating food from the trash cans behind restaurants and water from public restrooms. Each day was a grueling battle inside my head. Afraid of going home. Afraid to face life. Afraid to accept that I was alive on this planet. Afraid of what everyone would say when they saw me again. I wallowed in my despair, day in, day out, mentally spiraling growing crazier as the days went on. My heart ached to see Elena and everyone again. Dreams of the first time I met Elena back in Biology class. Dreams that flared into nightmares, always ending in with everyone fielding away, just as my father did, just as those students had on the mountain.

I finally reached my breaking point and couldn't stand this pain any longer. I needed to move on, to leave town and leave this life behind me. But before I could, I knew I had to remove any reason for returning. And so I found a nearby car and smashed its window. I hopped into the driver's seat and, using a little trick I had learned with my father when I was younger, I hotwired the car and steered towards my old campus.

I drove around the campus I once called home, keeping my head low to avoid unwanted attention. It had been weeks since the accident, but still, the town felt cold and lifeless. As the final classes of the day let out, I kept my eyes open for Elena. I parked my car across the road from where her last class let out. Students filed out of the building. After a couple of minutes of waiting, she finally came out. As she stepped out of the building, I found myself reminiscing about the first time I saw her. She looked just as beautiful as the first time I saw her. It started lightly raining as she started walking home. I followed her back to our house, trailing her in the car. When I was certain that no one else was around, I sped the car up, pulling over next to the sidewalk she was on. She looked in through the passenger side window. Her face showed confusion and disbelief. I unlocked the door and waved to her to open it. She opened the door and cautiously took a seat.

"Where have you been? Are you ok? You look like you haven't had a shower in forever. Whose car is-"

I cut her off. "Let's take a drive, and I will explain everything."

I drove us around the area while I answered her questions. I took special care to take the roads less traveled to minimize our chances of being seen. I was honest with her, answering every question she threw my way truthfully. All except for one question.

"So where are we going?" She asked.

I hoped she wouldn't ask, but I knew deep in my heart it was bound to come up. I continued to drive without response. She decided to let it go. I stopped the car in an empty parking lot at a rundown and abandoned hiking trail.

"Alright, I'm serious now. Where are we?" she said, sounding annoyed now.

My heart was racing now, just as it had when I asked her out on our first date. The rain continued outside, tapping on the roof of the car. I needed to get her out of my life for good. I loved her, and it was that love that kept me trapped. I couldn't take the pain anymore, the same overwhelming emotion I felt when I had slammed my fist onto that locker returned. Just as I struck that locker weeks ago, I struck Elena across her temple. My knuckles opened a gash across her forehead. Blood started streaming down her face. Her eyes widened, and I struck her again. This time, instead of feeling pain and sorrow, I felt relief. Relief from all the pain.

Her unconscious body slammed back against her seat.

I stepped out of the car and locked her inside. I took the key and dropped it into the gas tank. I then pulled a lighter out of my pocket and threw it in too. Within an instance, the car was engulfed in fire that danced through the cabin of the car. Her unconscious body lay there, unaware that soon, she would burn to a crisp. I watched as the blood on her head rapidly dried. I watched as her skin tightened around her body, constricting her. Her body curled into a ball as the temperature rose. What I thought may be difficult to watch soon became enjoyable, exciting even. As the car was completely engulfed in flames, I found myself smiling. Goosebumps arose on my arms. For so much of my life, I was afraid of death. I was surrounded by death. This feeling of loss plagued my mind. But now in this moment, as Elena's body turned to a dark crust, I felt what I can only describe as love. A love for fear. A love for death. A love for murder. A love this strong must be retracted, and so, I set my eyes towards my next victim.

-The Hunter

Dear Detective Leo,

I continued to sleep under people's houses at night and steal food from dumpsters. I even broke into another car, this time a green 1968 Mustang. It has been days since I had set Elena ablaze. Ever since, I have been itching. Each day, I feel as though thousands of spiders are biting me. For the longest time, I had been trapped in strands of webbing that connected together in a beautiful ornate pattern. I felt comfort in that web, it held me tight, like my mother used to, but when I killed that first time, I was no longer trapped. I was no longer scratching at each bite. I was no longer the prey. I was the spider, the hunter, if you will, capturing my victims in a web of nightmares. With my newfound love, I strung my next plan together.

Much like Elena, Barb was a well-liked and talented individual. The type of person in school that knew everyone's name and smiled at everyone. The type of person who would volunteer her afternoons to help clean the beaches. Someone who everyone considered to be a future leader, someone who would fight for everyone and everything. She was a beacon of hope. However, this future would never come.

I had watched Barb from afar since that first killing. I've watched her degrade as she deals with the death of her best friend. I watched her as every night, she'd drive off to a private beach that only our friends knew about. I watched her every night as she looked at the sunset over the water. One night, I finally decided to strike. It was near the golden hour. The ground was illuminated by the fading rays of the sun. She had gone to our group's favorite bar that night. I watched as she stumbled into her car and took off into the sunset. I followed suit, taking every twist and turn as she did. I watched as her car drifted slightly from left to right on the narrow roads. With each twist and turn, my skin began to itch once again. After thirty or so minutes, she turned off onto the nearby shoulder. The road was lined with trees on both sides. She exited the car and shuffled through a manmade trail that led to a nearby rock at the edge of the trees and sandy beach. She took a seat and stared into the sunset. Her silhouette sat centered inside of the sun. I wondered to myself what she might be thinking about. What would her last few thoughts be before her life was taken? Would they be about her friends? Maybe her family? Perhaps it would be about the sun. Whatever it was, it wouldn't matter. I watched as the sun set over her hunched body. As her shadow elongated as the sun lowered into the horizon, I stepped out of my car.

Her shadow began to be absorbed by the night light. I crept silently towards her like a spider approaching their prey. I felt the ground change from its dark asphalt to damp dirt. I brushed past the tree line slowly so as not to announce my presence. The ground then shifted from the damp dirt to a now soft yellow sand. With each step, my feet gently sunk into the ground. I was behind her now. I lifted my leg, and with all my might, I launched my foot deep into her back, knocking her from the rock. She turned on the ground, gazing up at me now in the moonlight. She looked at me with confusion and bewilderment. Her eyes widened as she recognized my face, but before she could say a word. I grabbed her head and stabbed it into the rock. She must have been knocked unconscious after the first blow, but I wasn't done. I slammed her head against the rock. With each blow, you could hear her skull change from a solid thud to a mushy goo. Blood painted the rock to a deep, dark red. I continued to slam her head against the rock. With each blow, I became more and more excited. I started experimenting with my technique, now testing different angles and trying to drag her face across the jagged edges of the rock.

I continued this process till her face was unrecognizable. I grabbed her feet and dragged her body across the sand, leaving a trail of blood that had clumped together in the sand. I chucked the lifeless corpse into the waves. I watched as her body drifted off into the ocean. As the next day's sun began to rise, I walked back to my car with a smile on my face.

-The Hunter

Dear Detective Leo,

The college is a ghost of what it once was. It's a husk of what it once was. Students drag their feet from building to building. Not real zombies of course, but ghosts of people who have lost a part of themselves. A community so tightly woven together, now shuffling through each day. Everyone except for one. One person has seemingly fallen off the face of the earth. Cal has locked himself in the house we once shared.

Ever since I met Cal in elementary school, he has been a tightly wound ball of stress, waiting to unravel. Growing up in a small town had its ups and downs. Being able to walk across town and recognize everyone you crossed paths with was a nice feeling. It made you feel like you were more than just another stranger on the street. However, even though everyone knew each other by name, I found challenges making many friends. It wasn't every day you found someone who knew the names of every named character in Star Wars. That was until one day at recess, Cal approached me and complimented my favorite Star Wars shirt. That simple comment was the spark that ignited a friendship that I have always cherished.

Cal was a very sweet soul. He was the type of person who would give you their umbrella in the rain and only allow half of the umbrella to cover them, just so you could stay dry. If you had dropped your books on the ground, he was the type of person to stop everything he was doing to help you pick them up. He was a pure and wholesome person, but he also had a different side to him. As stated, Cal was a nervous wreck. Many times, when we would spend nights at each other's houses for sleepovers, you would hear him thrashing about in his sleep. If you listened closely enough, you could from time to time hear him murmur words such as "the dark." Sometimes, he would even snap awake in the night screaming.

After moving in together with Elena and Barb, he would confess to me that he had nyctophobia, the fear of being in the dark. This fear that nearly every child in existence has experienced and then overcome to some extent was the same fear that caused my friend's life to be in near constant fear. He confessed to me that a certain part of him dreaded when I would come over and stay the night because that would mean he would have to sleep without his nightlight. I found this humorous as now we were both college students, afraid of failing a class or doing poorly on a quiz.

It had been seven days since I killed Barb, and another four since I killed Elena. I sat in a stolen car at midnight, parked across the street from where we all once lived. Cal sheltered himself inside of the house, alone. No roommates to talk to. No friends to confide in. Just empty rooms, collecting dust. He locked all the doors and went the extra mile to board up the windows. The house looks straight out of a Halloween horror movie. Each day since Barb, my body has continued to burn. I became more anxious than ever. Voices shouted throughout my mind, telling me it was time. I listened to the voices and stepped out of the car. I swung a backpack over my shoulders and cautiously walked up the front porch steps, trying not to make a noise. I reached the top of the steps, dug my hand into my back pocket, and pulled out my old house key. I inserted the key into the knob and twisted it. I haven't been in this house in ages. I wonder if the house has changed since the death of Elena and Barb.

I turned the knob and swing the door open, trying not to make too much noise. As soon as the door opened, my nose was assaulted with what I can only describe as a burning electrical smell and an old library. It was a very odd smell, but I pushed the thought away, not thinking anything of it. As I first stepped into the house, I felt my shoe catch on something sticky. I looked down to see that the entire floor had been covered with newspaper clippings and glue.

I read the headlines. Nine found dead on Mt. Hood. Local student found burned alive in a stolen vehicle. Another local student found dead floating in the ocean.

I smirked to myself before standing back up and continuing my way into the house. I reached for the light switch. When I flicked the switch, though, I felt a cool liquid-like substance on the switch. Confused by the sensation and how the lights didn't turn on, I took a step back to think. I decided not to waste time figuring out why the lights didn't work and opened a nearby closet. I remember placing a flashlight in the closet when we all first moved in, in case the lights ever stopped working. I turned the flashlight on and illuminated the walls. I glanced at the light switch again, somewhat curious as to what substance might have been. As I flashed the wall I saw long streaks of deep dark blood that trailed its way down the and around the main hallway. The blood was in a vicious-like state, not yet dried, but still liquid nonetheless. I looked around the corner, following the trail of blood. I peered down the long hallway. The pictures at once hung on the walls, now laid flat on the ground, shattered and bloodied. I turned my flashlight to the ceiling. Spider webs hung from the corners, creating a sort or archway. I noticed that the light bulbs had been removed. If it wasn't for this flashlight, everything would have been pitch black. That is, except for one dim light at the end of the hallway coming from the study.

I began my way down the hallway, walking cautiously. I first passed my old room. I tried opening the door, but it had been locked. Not wanting to risk making too much noise, I moved on. I passed Barb's old room. Her room was also locked, but the door had a hole in it. It looked as if someone had punched a hole through the thin wooden panel. I looked through the hole to see the room completely untouched. I turned back down the hall and continued my search. I next came to Cal's room. Unlike the others, the door to his room was wide open. The floor had a layer of opened and unopened boxes of light bulbs. Some boxes had been drenched in blood, others in perfect condition. I stepped out of the room and continued my way towards the light. I passed one final room before entering the study.

The door to Elena's room was cracked open. I pushed the door open and walked inside. Just as Barb's room was left untouched, so was Elena's. Her room was just as it looked when I had seen it last. A brief wave of warmth came over me as I remembered the feeling of her touch. For a brief moment, I felt a sense of regret, but that quickly disappeared as that same warmth turned into a burning sensation. I was then reminded of the joy I felt as I watched her skin turn black and tighten to her bones. Before I left her room, I looked towards her bed. Atop her sheets lay her diary.

Every day without you is torture. I feel as if a part of me is trying to escape from inside. It scratches at my ribcage, begging to be let out, but I can never leave. I miss you. I am trapped inside a cage without you. Please come back to me. - Elena, 6/6/1993.

It was the date I killed her. My nose scrunched, and my eyebrows lowered. I slammed the book closed and stormed out of the room. I was back in the hallway. I turned towards studying. I walked towards the door and I heard a noise coming from the other side. I knew I had found my next victim. I opened the door and peeked inside. I saw him seated at his large, handcrafted desk. His body slouched over the desk with his head buried in his arms. I quietly approached him so as not to alert him. The desk had a thin layer of dust over top of it. A pool of blood had formed around his arms. You could hear him whimpering to himself. I took a seat in front of the desk. As I sat down, the chair let out a loud creek. It was then when Cal's head jolted upwards. And that was when I saw what he had become. Cal had gouged his own eyes out and replaced the empty sockets with light bulbs. Blood streamed down his face like tears. The blood stood out prominently against his pale skin from the lack of blood. I spoke up with a hint of fear in my voice, officially revealing my presence.

"What happened to this place? What happened to you?" I asked while I watched the blood run down his face and neck.

Cal cleared his throat and spoke, "I knew my time would come. I never expected it to come from someone like you, though... I've been afraid of the dark all my life. I was afraid that I was being watched from the shadows, that there was something sinister plotting to hurt me... I knew that when Barb was killed after Elena something was going on. I knew that this was planned... I locked myself in this house with the lights on at all times... But It wasn't enough. Despite my best efforts, I realized the only darkness left to get rid of was the darkness I saw when I closed my eyes." he pulled a spoon from his pocket. "I thought if I simply replaced my eyes with the light, that I would never see the dark again... But now everything is dark. I can't escape this endless void. Please, help me see the light again."

"How am I supposed to help you?" I responded.

"Show me the light again., he said in a ghastly voice.

I grew impatient with Cal. I have been waiting for this kill for days. I reached inside my backpack and grabbed a club. I swung the bat across the side of his face, shattering the lightbulbs. He fell to the ground. I grabbed his legs and dragged him outside to the front side of my car. I propped him up against the front bumper. I then popped open the hood of the car and grabbed the jumper cables from the backseat. I clamped the cables to the battery and then clamped the other end to Cal's hands. It was time to show him the light once again. I sat down in the driver's seat and turned the key. The car shuttered as the engine started. I then turned the engine off and on again... and again... and again. With each turn of the key, his body shook and spazzed as the electricity coursed through his veins. The air smelled of metal and burnt flesh. I turned the key again. Cal violently thrashed as each volt attacked his body. I turned the engine off one final time and walked to his corpse. As I stood over his dead body, I saw the lightbulbs flicker in his eyes and a smile across his face.

-The Hunter

Dear Detective Leo,

Now you have heard my detective story. I've told you my past. I've given you a look inside my head, a peek into the madness. I bring you one step closer to the truth through each of these letters. One step closer to me. But why would I do this? Why would I help a detective solve the murders I have committed? The reason is simple—the thrill of the hunt! For so long, for so many years, I have been The Hunter. I have stalked my prey, watched them, followed them, planned my attack, and the ever-so-satisfying kill. I wish to give you that same thrill. I have lived free for decades, waiting, longing for someone to catch onto my trail, but no one has caught on. I've grown impatient, and because of this, I've chosen you. You, the newest and brightest detective on the force. I want to give you the opportunity to start your career with a bang. But be warned, every mistake you make will cost you something dearly. Good luck, Detective Leo, and happy hunting.

-The Hunter (and Prey)

NOTHING

ALLYSON STADELMAN

I am afraid
of nothing, knowing
nothing, feeling
nothing, the absence
of connection, accomplishing
nothing, doing
nothing, spending time
without productivity, nothing
is deceitful, a spider's
web, I'm entranced
by its strands, engulfed
in its grip, nothing
consumes me,
extracting my ability
to move, afraid
if I fall
into nothing,
I will become
nothing

BECAUSE YOU WON'T BE HERE FOR MY GRADUATION

MEGAN FARMER

CONTENT WARNINGS:
Discussions of death

Hey Grandpa,

It's fall at Pacific again, and I've been thinking a lot about you, because the last time I spent a fall semester at Pacific was two years ago, and you were alive. A lot has happened since then. I acted in that play that I was upset about my part in and made the best of it. I dedicated it to you. I studied in Ireland, like we talked about in our last conversation. I dreamed about you almost every night for the first couple of months. My friends and I were walking around Limerick one day when I saw these fishing lures in a museum gift shop, and I thought about how they would have been the perfect gift for you.

We sold your old house, and Grandma moved into town with Aunt Shirley. We've been trying to take her out to do things. It took us a long time to go through the house. You had a lot of stuff. We had an estate sale, and you would have hated it. All those people in your house, going through your stuff. We kept Dad in the garage the whole time, selling your old tools, and he kept losing his patience with people, eventually just telling them to get lost if they kept trying to haggle. You would think that the fact that it was an "estate" sale would make people nicer, but that was very much not the case. In their defense, there were a lot of treasures in that house.

They finally buried Grandma's brother that summer after his wife passed. They're in a plot together in a military cemetery. My brother was up that week and we'd planned on spreading your ashes, but we just couldn't do it. I don't know when we will. I don't know if we ever will. I think a part of dad is still mad that you didn't want a funeral. I think a part of me is still upset you didn't want an obituary.

Mom's sister passed while I was in Ireland, so we're helping raise her grandkid. For her memorial, we put her ashes in bubbles and spread them at the hippy fair over the summer. We even got dad to go. He wore shorts and a tie-dyed shirt, if you can believe it. His best friend passed over the summer. We drove the lead truck in the funeral procession. It was quite the turnout. It made me wonder what yours would have been like.

Sometimes, when I start to tally up the years and think about everyone that's gone now, it feels a bit like the world goes into slow motion. Like trying to move through water. One of my fiction professors has this lesson she teaches her intro students called the swimming pool analogy. She says that you have to provide context and background for your story, but your story is a swimming pool. If you spend too long stopping in the past, the reader will get bogged down and drown. I think that life is like that too. You have to look back, it's good to. But if you let it get to you too much, you drown in the story.

It's my senior year this year. I'm applying to grad schools now. I'm even looking at one in West Virginia. I was thinking the other day about how your mom never got the chance to learn to read or write, and how you got that award in the second grade for reading four books. How you wound up in the military because everyone was in the military, and your other option was coal mining and you weren't going to do that. I thought about how dad dropped out his junior year of high school and never finished, but owns every Stephen King book. About how now I'm applying to Ph.D. programs in literature.

I got better being alone after you died. I had two weeks between when you passed and when I had to be back at Pacific, and we all tried to go back to normal.. I started driving around a lot. There was one day I drove myself out to the beach. I stopped at my favorite coffee shop and got a Snickers mocha, like you and grandma used to get. I went to Sunset beach, where we used to picnic, and leaned against my car and watched the waves and let myself think about nothing. It was January, but it was a sunny day. For those two weeks after you died, it was sunny almost every day.

Dad told me that on one of your drives towards the end, you'd told him that when I was born, you didn't think you'd live to see me graduate high school. But you did. You got to watch me start college, and make friends, and be brave enough to even apply for my study abroad. And you worried, along with everyone else, that I wouldn't be able to handle it, though you were far too nice to say it.

When I first thought you were going to die, I cried all night about all the things you wouldn't see me do. How you wouldn't see me graduate college, or get married, or have kids. How you wouldn't see me settle into life, or travel, or hear about any of the wonderful things that might happen. But I don't think that's true. I was playing my ukulele earlier today, feeling angsty and anxious and antsy, and singing this song that mentions West Virginia and always makes me think of you. I sang the part about wishing I'd listened more when you spoke, and the lights in the room flickered. The world has a way of reminding me you're still speaking.

I still put my coffee in the front cupholder whenever I'm the one driving, because driver gets the front cupholder. And I get Keebler Cheese and Cheddar Crackers when I need a pick-me-up. I order biscuits and gravy on special occasions and get a large thing of french fries whenever I go to KFC. I smile when I hear about baseball or *Gunsmoke*, and remember that last time you were in the hospital whenever I see little plastic condiment packets, like the one I helped you open. I picture a house whenever I drive by that valley you used to like, right on the hill you wanted to build one on.

Do you remember when we got that package from Virginia after your last brother died? Before we opened it, you joked that it made you nervous, a package from back South from an unknown sender. You said you thought the law might have finally caught you. I think after all those years, you were probably pretty safe, Grandpa Moonshine. When we did open the package, what we actually found was a picture. A picture of you as a little boy, that your brother carried with him in his wallet when he went to fight in WWII. Dad always says that I've learned more about you and grandma than he ever did, but it still shocks me sometimes how little of your life I really know. I'd never thought too much about your siblings, because you never spoke about them, and I'd never met them. I think I just assumed that meant you weren't close.

I remember that I thought I wanted to stay sad forever when you died. That something felt wrong about moving on. But I did, eventually. We all do one day. I know it probably doesn't seem like it, being as I cried writing this. But I smiled too. Apparently, the two things can coexist. There is still a grief there, always will be. But there's a hope there too.

I wrote a lot about grief and ghosts after you died,

and I never really stopped. I'm studying ghost stories now, looking at the ways that ghosts help us make sense of the world. How they help us to move on. I thought that it would be weird and niche and personal, that no one would really get it. Yet when I suggested hauntings as a theme for this book for my class, everyone agreed. Maybe we all just need to spend more time thinking about our ghosts.

I miss you. I love you. I'm doing alright.

I had this dream while I was in Ireland, that you died so I could fly. We were in a swimming pool, and I wanted to spring into the air, and you didn't have the energy to lift me but you pretended like you did. So you used the last of your energy, and you threw me into the air and I was flying. Everyone behind me yelled that I had killed you, but when I turned around, all I could see was that you were smiling.

AUTHOR BIOGRAPHIES

THOMAS ALEJANDRO is a guy who loves a good story, whether it be a film, a television show, a book, or a video game. The characters and the world fueled only by one's imagination has always fascinated him. Nourished by this love, he crafted a story, world, and characters of his own with only one goal in mind, to tell an amazing story meant for everyone and one that all can enjoy.

EMMA BLACKWELL was raised in Hillsboro Oregon. She graduated from Hillsboro High in 2022, and is student at Pacific University where she is double majoring in English Literature and Creative Writing. Her parents, Russ and Kristin Blackwell and her younger brother, James have played a major role in her life about finding what she wants to bring to the world. Emma wants to bring people closer to writing and the art of storytelling, and how finding that one story that you truly reside with will bring a whole new outlook on life.

JEANRI BOSCH (she/her) is loving the rainy season, and she's loving the warm and cozy mornings where she can stay in bed. She's a bit stressed and confused about what life holds for her after graduation. As a Fine Art major and Computer Science minor, she doesn't quite know which direction to go in yet. But she knows she'll be getting a cat and maybe more piercings.

ALIZAH CARRILLO is a chemistry major studying at Pacific University. She was born in Maui, Hawaii. Art is one of the many hobbies she picked up from her childhood, ranging from watercolors to digital art.

KAYANAH COOPER is a creative young woman with mixed feelings about people and the world. She often tries to see the best in people but finds it especially difficult to force herself to go at the same pace as her peers. She enjoys making art and raising little dragons on her phone and playing Monopoly. She wants to have a big birthday party someday but she has no idea what that even means. She's consistently broke and simultaneously buying everything she wants with no hesitation. She wants to change her hair color but change alone scares her.

JACKLYN-DIANA DUREKE is an accounting major and international studies minor. She enjoys being a nail tech, trying new restaurants, and spending time with her friends and family.

MEGAN FARMER studies literature and creative writing at Pacific University. When she was a child, she was obsessed with cemeteries. She now spends her time studying and writing ghost stories, and telling anyone who will listen about one of her favorite places to visit in Ireland: Glasnevin Cemetery in Dublin.

QUINTANA FRANKLIN is a lover of the morbid and ghastly. 85% of her wardrobe is black and she prefers spending time with animals instead of people. She enjoys creating art through movement as a way of sharing her stories and communicating with the world. She studies kinesiology because she thinks the human body is neat and she enjoys escaping the real world through fiction.

CHEYENNE GARDNER (they/them) is a queer college student who enjoys hanging out with their pet mouse and fiancé, going on mini adventures, and wrapping the interior of their apartment with festive lights.

CAROLINE HILL (she/her) is a lover of the outdoors. She enjoys cozy blankets, reading, and exploring new places. She is in her third year of studying psychology. She is often found in the library next to a big window sipping chai.

ROBYN HOLLEY is a cross-country transplant from the semi-fictional town of Lyndeborough, New Hampshire where she began writing stories about a colorful sasquatch character called the Squambat. Robyn now lives in the Portland area with her beloved Darren, their very good doggie Huxley, and their mischievous ginger cat Tibby. When she isn't taking blurry photographs of the elusive Squambat, Robyn avoids her homework by focusing on beading, knitting, making dragon eggs, and wrestling with her ding-danged sewing machine. She studies anthropology at Pacific University and dreams of going on archaeological digs and practicing cultural resource management.

DAWSON HOSE' is a Computer Science Major. He enjoys being with friends and is currently on the Men's tennis team.

ZAK KLEMP is a college student who is planning on following in his mother's footsteps as an educator. At night, he teaches Taekwondo classes to his amazing students. He loves to spend time watching movies or shows with his family or to simply lay in his bed while listening to music or playing dumb games. He also wants readers to know that writing this piece was a wonderful experience that has haunted him at night.

REIGEN KOMAGATA is currently a sophomore here at Pacific University. He was born and raised in Aiea, Hawaii on the island of Oahu. Reigen is planning on double majoring in Criminal Justice Law & Society and Philosophy. If there is one thing that Reigen wants for you to take away from this bio is that the sooner you fall behind, the more time you have to catch up. So, if someone askes you if it is "due tomorrow," just reply with "do tomorrow," and always remember that if you procrastinate you'll never be bored because there is so much that you could be doing.

SOPHIA LEWIS has always dreamed of being a published author, but she struggles to write and hates sharing her work. She's always feared slimy things, but recently held a snake for the first time and found that it wasn't slimy at all. With that revelation in mind, she's now ready to conquer the world—aka publish a book.

CRYPTID PARKE is a creative writing and editing & publishing student who intends to be come a professor. Their work focuses primarily on the places people inhabit and what it means to exist in time and space. Cryptid enjoys looking at the world through a gothic lens to reveal the horror beneath the surface, and often uses their experiences growing up in the Midwest as fodder for their love of magical realism. When not writing, they can be found curled up on the couch with their cat, Soup, listening to a podcast.

KAYLA PASKEWICH (She/They) is an artist and a Social Work Major, spends most days inside her tiny dorm doing homework instead of enjoying her hobbies. When not overloaded with mountains of work, she enjoys drawing on her iPad, watching Better Call Saul with her partner, snuggling with a long-haired German Shepherd named Mercy, and spending time photographing out in nature. She also partakes in the art of finding cheap thrifted clothing, putting in hours to make a 200+ song Spotify playlist, and spending too much time researching a various hyperfixations.

RILEY REYNOLDS is a creative writing major who has an unhealthy obsession with D&D as well as other TTRPG systems. Outside of these intrests he runs his own graphic clothing business with the goal of paying off his student loans.

DREW SHERMAN lives a quiet life full of explosions and high energy action. After a long day of saving the world he hangs his hat and focuses on the simple things in life like rocket science. After hours of grueling and selfless world saving he trains to be the first man to make the Kessel Run in less than 12 parsecs.

GRACIE SHOEMAKER is a sophomore at Pacific University. She is studying Creative Writing, as well as Editing and Publishing. She grew up with ghosts in her house, and manages to find new ones everywhere she goes. When she's not talking to the ghosts of her half-written stories, she's busy getting excited about a new hobby that will barely last longer than a week.

ALLYSON STADELMAN is a kinesiology major with a passion for dance. Music fuels her soul, she rarely sits in silence. She loves plants, her pets, and sweet treats. When she isn't dancing or studying she likes to spend her time outside. She enjoys hiking and nature photography. Her day is not complete without a caffeinated drink.

HALEY TAYLOR is studying creative writing at Pacific University. When she doesn't have her nose stuck in a book, she enjoys riding rollercoasters as many times as possible, taking way too many pictures, and crushing her friends in Mario Kart Wii. She is currently working on a novel that she can't summarize, so don't ask her to.

TERYN TOMINAGA is a Literature major with a planned minor in Creative Writing and Japanese. Her favorite authors are J.K. Rowling, Douglas Preston, and Lincoln Child. Although she does believe Rick Riordan, Brandon Mull, and Brandon Sanderson deserve honorable mentions. In her spare time she kicks herself out the door to go running because she knows she'll feel content afterwards. And of course she also loves to read. As far as writing goes, the love-hate relationship she has with it produces pieces she obsesses over and seeks much validation from, as well as pieces she reads and questions how stupid her past self could be. She loves listening to music, always trying to discover new genres, sounds, and voices. She hates gnats- what exactly do they do that's of any significance?- and how it suddenly becomes extremely difficult to wake up before eight (before twelve really) when in college. She hopes the readers enjoy this anthology.

MAGGIE TRABOSH is the older, but shorter sister. She watches way too much reality tv, and eats a lot of Mac and cheese. She always wears a ring from her mom, and her best friend is a stuffed giraffe. She gets very winded going up stairs and yet has a huge fear of elevators. She likes oversized sweatshirts, free socks, and the same pair of shoes that she's owned for years.